PUCK AHOLIC

A BAD MOTHERPUCKERS NOVEL

LILI VALENTE

SELF TAUGHT NINJA PUBLISHING

All Rights Reserved

Copyright **Puck Aholic** © 2017 Lili Valente

All rights reserved. Without limiting the rights under copyright reserved above, no part of this publication may be reproduced, stored in or introduced into a retrieval system, or transmitted, in any form, or by any means (electronic, mechanical, photocopying, recording, or otherwise) without the prior written permission of the copyright owner. This erotic romance is a work of fiction. Names, characters, places, brands, media, and incidents are either the product of the author's imagination or are used fictitiously. The author acknowledges the trademarked status and trademark owners of various products referenced in this work of fiction, which have been used without permission. The publication/use of these trademarks is not authorized, associated with, or sponsored by the trademark owners. This e-book is licensed for your personal use only. This e-book may not be re-sold or given away to other people. If you would like to share this book with another person, please purchase an additional copy for each person you share it with, especially if you enjoy hot, sexy, emotional romantic comedies featuring alpha males. If you are reading this book and did not purchase it, or it was not purchased for your use only, then you should return it and purchase your own copy. Thank you for respecting the author's work. Cover design by Bootstrap Designs. Editorial services provided by Help Me Edit.

❦ Created with Vellum

ABOUT THE BOOK

I hate my new roommate.

And I want to do dirty, delicious things to her in that swing she installed that we both know has *nothing* to do with aerial yoga.

Neither of which is good, considering Diana Daniels is my NHL team captain's little sister, and he *will* break my face if I'm not a perfect gentleman.

I try to be. Really, I do. But when Diana runs screaming down the hall wearing nothing but a damp washcloth, all my gentlemanly intentions go out the window. She's got all sorts of Jedi mind tricks to make a man obsessed with getting her into bed, and I'm not gonna lie—I fall for every single one of them.

ABOUT THE BOOK

Especially the one where she warns me not to fall for her.

* * *

Everyone knows that banging your new roomie is a bad idea. And if it wasn't for his sister's stupid pet pig, Wanda, chasing me out of the bathroom mid-shower, Tanner Nowicki and I might still be able to pretend we hate each other.

But that pig totally has it out for me, and before I can warn Tanner that I don't do relationships—or hockey players or my brother's friends, for that matter—he's doing *me*. Against the wall. And in his bed. And in my bed. And on a pinball machine where we get an all time high score.

And it's so incredible that I start to forget that I'm the unluckiest woman alive when it comes to relationships. And pigs. And aerial yoga. And worst of all, love.

But hey, it's not like I didn't warn him…

*Dedicated to Lucky, who taught me just how
irritated an animal can get when his humans are
publicly displaying their love.
Dad and I apologize for disgusting you and
are so glad we have a pup like you to keep us in line.*

CHAPTER ONE

TANNER AKA NOWICKI

Tonight, I helped a friend propose to the woman he loves. I made two people who are perfect for each other very happy, solidified a bond with a teammate I admire, and got to watch the sunset from the deck of a multimillion-dollar beachside mansion where I'll be spending the night with a group of good friends and their families.

I finally made the list. I'm a "cool kid."

As a rookie, there was a time—like two months ago—when I didn't get invited to the smaller, veteran parties, the private gatherings of the players who know they've got a home in Portland as long as they stay fast and refrain from getting their heads slammed into the glass too often. Concussions take out a lot of good players before their time.

And then there are guys like me, whose brains are hardwired wrong from the get-go. I finished the season strong, and my contract was renewed for next year, but if I don't keep my focus laser-sharp, I might not be a Badger for long.

It's best that I don't get attached. Don't get in too deep. Don't allow myself to wish I wasn't at this party alone.

I don't have time for a girlfriend, and I'm in no place to make a long-term commitment.

But as I watch my teammates pair off with their significant others—wandering down to the darkened beach or up to their rooms—I can't help feeling low.

And cranky.

And a little jealous.

Fine, a lot jealous. Until this year, I haven't spent much time alone. I've always had a girlfriend or a steady date on the verge of becoming a girlfriend. I like women, get along well with the better-smelling sex, and enjoy spending time with humans who aren't afraid to talk about things other than sports or work, which happen to be the same in my world, further reducing the opportunities for conversational variety.

And then there's sex…

I sigh heavily as I plod down the stairs toward the beach, my flask of whiskey in hand.

God, I fucking miss fucking. I miss it so much I'm starting to wonder if there's something wrong with me.

Surely even the most testosterone-fueled meatheads don't think about sex as much as I think about sex. And the only thing that keeps me from dwelling on how long it's been since I had a woman in my bed—seven months, three days, and a handful of hours—is killing myself on the ice at practice and pushing myself to the limit during every game.

But now I have a four-week hiatus until practices officially start again, and nothing but my morning workouts, a few scrimmages, and a charity event to keep my thoughts out of the gutter.

Summer hookup, man.

There's nothing wrong with something temporary as long as you're up front with the girl about what you're up for and what you're not.

I tip back my flask, sending more Johnny Walker Blue flowing into my mouth, so smoky and smooth there isn't a hint of burn when I swallow.

A summer hookup won't work. I know myself better than that. If I find a girl I like enough to want to fuck her, I'm going to want to keep fucking her and caring about her and moving forward until something eventually gets in the way. And if that something is me needing to end things because I can't keep my head in the game or I've been transferred to an armpit team in Arizona, I'll feel like an asshole.

"Alone," I mutter, lifting my flask to the black ocean waves crashing against the darkest, loneliest corner of the beach near the bluffs. The place where I clearly belong. "Better to go it alone."

The words have barely passed my lips when something warm and smelling pleasantly of musky campfire collides with my backside, sending me stumbling a few unsteady steps forward.

"Oh my God, I'm sorry!" A female giggle follows the apology, and a slim hand grips my arm. "Are you okay? Did I hurt you?" She giggles again, as if the idea of injuring strangers amuses her.

I smile, figuring it's time to lay off the whiskey if a collision with a kid half my size has me off balance. I can't see the girl's face well in the dim light from the sliver of a moon, but she's tiny, probably no more than sixteen or seventeen. "I'm fine. But should you be down here by yourself?"

"Should *you* be down here by yourself?" She brings a cigarette to her lips and inhales, making the tip flare. "I hear this beach has killer mermaids." She exhales, sending that musky, almost skunky smell drifting through the air again, and I realize that's no cigarette.

"Killer mermaids?" I ask, playing along. "Is that right?"

She nods. "Killer, carnivorous mermaids. And they like

guys like you most of all." She grips my arm again, giving my bicep a squeeze. "Mmm, yes, nice juicy muscles. So dee-lish-usssss…"

I flex beneath her touch because I am a man and it's hardwired into my DNA to flex like a cheesy bastard when someone fondles my muscles, even if the person feeling me up is a wasted teenager.

"Nice." She clucks her tongue as she squeezes my other arm. "Too bad you're going to be mermaid-bait pretty soon."

"So it's too late, you think? To make a run for safety?"

She nods with a heavy sigh. "Yes. Sadly, it's too late. They'll be here any second. Can't you hear them? Laughing in the waves?"

We both go silent for a moment, listening, then my wasted companion starts giggling again. "Sorry," she says, "That was me. Don't be afraid. That was me laughing."

"Yeah, I could tell." I arch an amused brow. "Maybe you should put that out and save the rest for later?"

"I'm sorry. Where are my manners?" She moves the blunt between us. "You want some? It's good. Smooth, not too heavy. Takes the edge off a shit start to the weekend."

"No thanks, I don't smoke," I say, beginning to think I've misjudged her age. Yes, she's petite, but her world-weary voice is pure disillusioned grownup. "I'm Tanner, by the way."

"Hey, Tanner." She accepts the hand I hold out, shaking it firmly. "You here for the party back there?"

"Yeah. You?" I wonder if she's someone's girlfriend then realize I don't like how that wondering makes me feel. I haven't even seen this woman—or girl, I'm still not sure—clearly, and I'm already starting to develop a crush.

Fuck, I need to get laid.

Or stop drinking whiskey.

Or both.

"Nah." She shakes her head, making her ponytail—blonde, I think, or light brown, and a little curly—swish. "Just here to help with a family thing. My brother's girlfriend proposed to him tonight and needed me to help facilitate the fucking romance."

I grunt. "That's crazy. My friend proposed to his girlfriend tonight, too. I was in charge of guarding the stairwell to make sure no one disturbed them until she said yes."

"And did she?"

"Yeah. How about your brother?"

She makes an exasperated growling sound. "Yes. And it was ridiculously romantic, and they cried because they're so happy and in love." She takes another pull on her joint, holding the smoke in as she adds, "If I didn't love them so much, I would have vomited. I'm so over happy couples right now. They're so fucking gross."

I grin. "They are kind of gross."

"Totally gross." She nudges me with her elbow. "So I guess you aren't living happily ever after?"

"Not currently. How about you?"

She snorts. "No. Not now, not ever. Ten years of trying, and all I've got to show for it is a handful of Mr. Wrongs and a Mr. Right I broke up with because I dated him too soon after Mr. Super Duper Wrong and was too stupid to see that I was running away from the best thing that had ever happened to me. And now he's engaged, too, and life is dumb, and I'm done with relationships. I'm probably going to move to Tibet and become a monk."

"Aren't monks men?"

"Yeah." She shrugs as she drops the nub her joint has become to the ground and toes sand over it. "I'll have to pretend to be a guy, I guess. But how hard can that be? Just cut my hair, drop my voice, walk funny, and check to make sure my dick is still there a lot. Easy."

I tilt my head, studying her face, which I'm able to see better now that wind has swept away the clouds that were muting the moonlight. She's pretty. Very pretty, with full lips that dominate her pixie face, and expressive eyebrows that make squiggles above her eyes as she asks, "What?"

"I think you might be too pretty to pull off pretending to be a guy. Sorry."

"You should be sorry. I hate it when sexy men with nice muscles tell me I'm pretty." She places a hand on my chest and leans in to add in a confidential whisper, "Just in case you're wondering, I'm hitting on you, and I think we should make out on the sand. What do you think?"

I blink, surprised, but not opposed to the idea, assuming…

"How old are you?" I step closer. If she's been dating for ten years, she's got to be at least in her early twenties, but it's better safe than sorry.

"Older than you are, Muscle Boy. Does that matter?"

"I'm twenty-four," I say, seriously doubting her claim. She looks twenty-one, maybe twenty-two, tops.

"Twenty-seven." Her arms go around my neck, and her breasts press against my chest, proving she's curvier than I thought, too. "Is that enough getting to know each other? Can we casually make out now?"

My lips part, but before I can speak, she's pushed up on tiptoe and pressed her lips to mine. And I don't know if it's the whiskey, or the dark beach and the crash of the waves, or the strange, yet oddly comforting, conversation—knowing I'm not the only one who's alone and not too pleased about it—but the kiss is…incredible.

She tastes like woodsy, slightly funky smoke, but sweet, too. A perfect mixture of bad influence and warm, sexy woman. And as we tumble to the sand, I find myself feeling happier than I have in a long time.

For what seems like hours, we kiss like teenagers—hot, hungry, hands roaming, but never slipping under clothes—before she whispers against my lips, "Thank you. I needed to touch someone tonight."

"You're welcome." My next words slip out before I can think better of them. "You can sleep over if you want. I'm staying at the house back there. King bed, plenty of room, no pressure to take things any further."

"Oh, Muscle Boy..." She sighs as her hand skims down my stomach to hover close to where my canvas shorts are strained at the front. Her fingers tease back and forth between my skin and the button holding the fabric closed, making the hard-on situation even more...pressing. "If I went back to your room, I would want a lot more than kissing."

"That's fine, too." All my promises not to start something this summer are forgotten as I imagine how good it's going to feel to make my beach pixie come and finally break my seven-month dry spell.

"No, it's not." She pulls out of my arms, moving to sit beside me on the sand. "I have to go home."

"I can call a car for you in the morning," I say. "First thing."

She shakes her head. "Can't. I'm moving tomorrow, and I still have to pack. My friend is coming to pick me up in half an hour. I promised her I would be out by noon. She's been cool about me crashing on her couch, but I'm sure she's sick of having my life exploded all over her living room."

I nod, crestfallen but trying not to show it. It's clear Beach Pixie's not interested in more than casual kisses and an easy "see ya later." But I can't seem to stop myself. "What about tomorrow night? Can I take you to dinner? Maybe bowling or something?"

She grins, sighing as she leans in, resting her head on my

shoulder. "Oh, you're sweet. Very, very sweet." She kisses my arm, right below where my T-shirt ends. "But I'm not that kind of girl anymore, Muscle Boy. You keep looking. Find yourself someone young and new, who isn't cursed with the worst love-life luck on the planet."

I start to protest—to tell her I'm not afraid of bad luck—but before I can speak, her lips are on mine. She kisses me again, until I'm even harder, aching, dying to roll her beneath me in the sand and make her feel so good she'll change her mind about staying with me tonight and dinner tomorrow.

But when I move to guide her on top of me, she pulls away, standing up and backing across the sand so fast she's already disappearing into the darkness when she says, "Good luck, Tanner. Thank you again."

Then she's gone, I'm alone, and suddenly the thought of waking up tomorrow surrounded by people in love is intolerable. With another pull on my flask, I head up the beach and march straight to my room, throwing my shit into my duffle as I call for a car. I rode here with Saunders and his girlfriend, but I'm sure they won't mind making the return trip alone.

Hell, they'll prefer it, no doubt.

No fucking doubt...

Just like there's no doubt that I'm never going to see my sexy beach pixie again. There are over half a million people in Portland. The chances of crossing paths with her are slim, and that's assuming she's staying in the area. She could be moving to another state for all I know. Another country.

An hour later, as I tumble into my bed at home, Pixie's already becoming part of the past, a memory touched by magic, a story I'll tell when I'm old. The entire encounter was a little too strange to be real. Maybe she was the ghost of a woman who drowned on that beach, or one of the killer mermaids she warned me about, come onto the shore to hunt for men stupid enough to wander too close to the waves.

For all I know, I could have barely escaped with my life.

The thought is ridiculous, childish even, but it makes the rejection sting less, and by the time I wake up the next morning I've all but forgotten about the girl I kissed last night.

When Brendan, my team captain, calls to tell me his little sister's new living situation fell through and ask if I'm still looking for a roommate, I don't for a single second consider that I might have met his sister before. That I might have kissed her, rocked against her through our clothes, wanted to make love to her more than I've wanted anything in a very, very long time.

I'm clueless, and say yes without thinking twice, not realizing what a serious mistake I've made until I open the front door an hour later to find Beach Pixie standing on my doorstep wearing tiny striped shorts, a tank top so thin it should be illegal, and a shocked expression that matches my own.

CHAPTER TWO

DIANA

*W*orst luck in the world.

I have the worst luck in the entire world.

What are the odds that the man I made out with on the beach last night—the one man in Portland, in fact, whose lips have met mine—would happen to be my brother's teammate and the only person in my small circle of friends who's looking for a roomie?

Slim, is the answer to that question. Very fucking slim.

Unless, of course, you are me and your bad luck is the legendary stuff of legend.

Shit sticks…

I should have stayed in bed this morning.

Maybe I would have if Carly's boyfriend Nick hadn't spilled his coffee on my head as he stumbled past the couch where I was sleeping—thankfully he likes it iced, not scalding —and awoken me with a cold caffeine shower from an X-rated dream starring Muscle Boy. And so far, the coffee bath has been the highlight of this day, polling above learning that the girl I paid a five-hundred-dollar deposit for the studio above her garage has run off to Mexico, leaving her parents (who actually own the house) to apologize profusely for their wayward loin-fruit and explain that the studio has already been rented to someone else, and standing on a stranger's doorstep hoping my luck is about to change only to be greeted by a shocked-looking Muscle Boy—who is even more handsome in the daylight than he was in the dim glow of the moon.

Handsome and clearly appalled by the sight of me.

As he should be. Because this here? This shacking up together in his cozy yellow bungalow? Well, that obviously is never going to fucking work.

"Hey, Nowicki." My brother trudges up the steps to the front porch behind me, carrying two heavy black cases filled with camera equipment that he will, unfortunately, soon be carrying right back to the car. "This is Diana, my oldest little sister. She moved to Portland a few weeks ago. Diana, this is Nowicki. He's a left wing, different line, just finished his rookie season."

"Actually we've—"

"Nice to meet you, Diana." Nowicki, aka Tanner—if my brother weren't a jock weirdo who refuses to use people's first names, this third disaster of the day could have been avoided—reaches out to clasp my hand. "I've heard good things."

"Really?" I frown as my fingers fold around his, ignoring how nicely warm and dry his palm is, and how tingle inducing it is to be touching him again.

So he wants to play it like this, does he? Pretend we've never met?

Why? Is he actually open to the possibility of living together? Or is he just afraid Brendan will pound his face if he finds out that Tanner and I were dry humping in the sand last night?

"Really." Tanner nods as he releases my hand. "Chloe showed me some of your shots. They're really good."

"Oh. Well...thank you." I arch a brow, taking in Tanner's slightly-too-wide eyes and the hint of perspiration beginning to dot his upper lip.

Yeah, it's definitely the second option. He fears a brother beating, which is amusing, considering Brendan is one of the kindest, most reasonable people I know and respects me enough to keep his nose out of my personal business. He always has, even when my personal business probably could have used some intervention.

"Where do you want me to put these, Nowicki?" Brendan asks from behind me. "Not to rush the introductions, but I'm pretty sure she's got her entire two-ton boulder collection in here."

"Right, sorry. Up the stairs, first door on the left." Tanner stands back, pulling the door open wider, revealing a beautiful open-concept living room that seamlessly flows into a sunny kitchen with antique cabinets and an old-fashioned refrigerator that is one of the more adorable things I've seen today.

And then a series of excited grunts sound from the other side of the room near the white brick fireplace, and I can't help but smile. There, with her pink-and-brown-spotted nose pressed to the gate of one of those free-standing pens made to corral dogs and toddlers, is the cutest damn miniature pig I've ever seen.

"Oh my God, she's a doll!" I float through the door and across the room, abandoning my duffle on the porch to keep my hands free for important things like scratching this beauty's chubby belly. I squat down at the gate, and Miss Adorable greets me with a fresh round of grunting. "What's her name?"

"Wanda," Tanner says from behind me. "But be careful. It

takes her awhile to warm up to strangers. She can be cranky with new people at first."

"No worries. Animals and I are all good." I wave away his concern with a flip of my wrist as I reach over the gate to stroke Wanda's lightly furred back. "It's humans you have to watch out for. Right, Wanda?"

The pig grunts again before retreating to the far side of her pen, where she roots beneath a large pink blanket until only her small, intelligent eyes and wiggling snout are visible at one end of her cover-cave.

"It's okay, sweets," I say. "I'm shy sometimes, too."

"And I'm the Queen of fucking England," Brendan mutters as he starts up the stairs. "Don't believe her for a second, Nowicki. That one doesn't have a shy bone in her body."

Tanner coughs, and I turn to see him watching me with a mixture of amusement and anxiety that is also pretty adorable. He's nearly as cute as his pig, but that doesn't matter. If we're going to do this roomie thing, we'll be doing it as friends, nothing more. And friends don't care if friends are tall, built like a brick house, or blessed with the sweetest set of dimples ever to grace a chiseled face.

"Wanda's why I need to find a roommate before the season starts again," Tanner says, motioning toward the snuggled-up pig. "I need someone to feed, walk, and play with her a couple times a day while I'm on the road for away games. But I'm assuming Brendan mentioned that?"

I nod. "He said there were some pet care responsibilities, and that was the reason the rent was so reasonable."

"Do you think you can handle that?"

"Like I said, I'm good with animals." I glance toward the stairs, making sure Brendan is out of earshot before I add in a softer voice, "But if we do this, we forget about last night, okay? Seriously. It's like it never happened."

Tanner steals a nervous glance over his shoulder. "That's a good idea no matter where you decide to live. Dating the relatives or exes of teammates is frowned on in Badger land."

Before I can assure him I'm not up for dating anyone, no matter what team they play for, Brendan tromps down the stairs, jabbing a thumb toward the second floor. "Go check out your new digs, Squirt. It's a sweet space. Lots of light, nice view of the backyard, and your own bathroom."

"Squirt?" Tanner echoes, grinning.

I point a stern finger at his chest. "That's for big brothers only. No one else gets to call me that."

"Except our sisters," Brendan adds, stopping beside Tanner. "Diana's the runt of the Daniels' litter."

"Shut up, Brendan," I warn, glaring at my brother.

But Brendan only laughs and slaps Tanner on the shoulder. "Help me grab the last of the bags? That way we can get them in one go and save the runt's tiny legs three or four trips up and down the stairs."

"Sure, happy to help," Tanner says, following my brother toward the still-open front door.

"Yeah, well, you guys may have gotten the brawn, but I got the brains," I call after them. It's been my standard comeback for short jokes since my teen years when it became clear I was going to spend the rest of my life looking up the nostrils of my siblings—both younger and older.

But to be honest, I'm not so sure about the state of my brain these days.

Maybe I shouldn't have resigned from the National Park Service, abandoning a quietly successful, albeit lonely, career as a nature photographer and non-profit PR consultant to try my luck in the big city. Maybe I should have stayed on the road, rolling from one federally-subsidized moldy cabin in the woods to the next until the day I got too old to hike up mountains to photograph bald eagle nests and retired to a tiny cottage I'd saved up enough to purchase after sixty years of pinching pennies and eating bulk granola for every meal.

Yes, it was poorly paid work, and grueling at times, but it was satisfying, peaceful, and familiar. I knew what to do when I ran into a bear with a newborn cub while roaming a trail, or got caught halfway up a cliff face in the middle of a thunderstorm. I have no idea what to do about lying city slickers stealing my money, public transportation that seems designed to confuse the hell out of me—despite Portland being named a top ten city for getting around without a car—or potential employers who are so profoundly disinterested in my resume they can't be bothered to confirm receipt of my emails.

So far, the transplant to the city isn't going nearly as smoothly as I'd hoped. And shacking up with a drop-dead gorgeous guy who I have no doubt would be a dynamite fuck buddy, is the very definition of Bad Idea.

It's been way too long since I let off that particular kind of steam, and as Tanner walks by with my duffle slung over one shoulder and my yoga bag hitched over the other, the sight of his hands on my things is enough to give me more bad ideas. Bad ideas that involve climbing Muscle Boy like a jungle gym and taking advantage of my new aerial-yoga-acquired flexibility to see how many ways we can get tangled up in each other before we collapse from exhaustion.

But I know how that would play out. Muscle Boy would end up being the latest in a long line of men who give new meaning to the word "douchebag," because no matter how hard I try to find a nice guy, I always end up attracting snakes, liars, losers, and sociopaths.

Or, I revise, as Tanner disappears up the stairs, gamely helping move in a roomie he had no idea was crashing his solitude until a couple of hours ago, he could prove to be every bit as nice as he seems. Given the chance, our instant chemistry might lead to something more, and then I would get to play the role of douchebag, because I'm never going to be good girlfriend material.

I've already had my "once in a lifetime" love, and I screwed it up. Now Sam is engaged to marry a beautiful humanitarian lawyer princess, and I'm going to spend the rest of my life alone. Because it's better to be alone than to play pretend with a man who deserves better than a girl who's always going to be hung up on the one who got away.

The one I *threw* away because I was too blind to realize that Sam was different, special, a diamond in a world full of...turds.

I wrinkle my nose, looking down to see Wanda letting loose a surprisingly large load of droppings for a mini pig, her bottom positioned so the turds tumble through the slats of her enclosure, leaving a revolting pile inches from my sandaled foot.

"I told you she takes a while to warm up to strangers," Tanner says, shaking his head as he surveys the present his little darling has left on the carpet.

I arch a brow. "You think this is a message for me?"

"Absolutely," he says. "She's crazy smart. Aren't you, Wanda?"

Wanda offers a series of musical grunts in response.

"Now go get a puppy pad so I can clean up your mess." Tanner props his hands on his hips. "Go get a puppy pad. Right now. You've been a bad pig. That's no way to welcome our new roomie."

After another grunting session that is decidedly more resentful in nature, the pig prances across her enclosure on dainty hooves, grabs a puppy pad from a stack of several, and trots back to Tanner with the absorbent sheet clenched between her teeth.

"You little brat." I laugh, not sure whether to be offended or impressed.

"This isn't a regular thing," Tanner assures me. "She's house-trained. She uses a puppy pad or goes outside unless she's trying to prove a point."

I cross my arms. "And her point is…?"

"That she considers you a threat," he says, his green eyes narrowing. "She isn't a fan of other women. But once she understands that you and I are just friends, she should settle down."

"So the pig is in love with you?" I grin up at him. "Is what you're saying?"

He shrugs. "The ladies love me, Diana. It's my cross to bear."

I'm still working up a comeback—too distracted by how nice my name sounds on Tanner's oh-so-kissable lips to be snappy with the repartee—when Brendan hustles down the stairs, waving an arm for help getting the last load from the back of the SUV.

I follow my brother outside while Tanner disposes of Wanda's welcome present. Even with a jealous pig and a dangerously sexy roommate to deal with, shacking up with Tanner is still preferable to letting Brendan install me in his guest room, the way he's been offering to do since I announced I was moving to Portland.

I don't want to horn in on his new family—he and his fiancée only moved in together six months ago—and I really don't want to wake up every morning and stumble down the stairs to see Brendan and Laura making goo-goo, lovey-dovey, smoochy-heart eyes at each other while they fix breakfast for my niece. I'm happy for them, I truly am, and I'm glad the dream is coming true for people I care about, but it's not easy to be around Happy Ever After Coupledom twenty-four hours a day, seven days a week.

In fact, it's flat-out nauseating.

I'll take pig droppings any day. At least until I can scour the message boards and find another affordable room for rent.

Decision made, I grab my laundry basket full of shoes from the back of the Trailblazer and head up the stairs, ready to make the best of my latest bout of bad luck. The one good thing about being the walking, talking, disaster-inclined proof of Murphy's Law is that I've learned to roll with the punches and get back on my feet without wasting time feeling sorry for myself.

And really, I observe, covertly admiring the view as Tanner bends over on the other side of the room, scrubbing the carpet with a sponge, things could be much worse.

Sure, I can't touch, but there are no rules against looking, and the scenery around this place is a truly beautiful thing.

CHAPTER THREE

TANNER

*A*ccording to the I.Q. tests they gave me as a kid—
back when my teachers were still trying to figure
out why I was struggling in school—I'm of above average
intelligence, though you wouldn't know it from the abundance of dumb decisions I've made in my life.

There was the time I ate a handful of Legos on a dare, the summer I decided jumping off the roof into a kiddie pool was a good idea, and the afternoon I ran away from my mom at the mall and spent the night locked in a storage room, certain I was going to die of starvation before someone found me. And then there was the time I skipped school with my girlfriend to take advantage of the fact that her parents were out of town on business, only to be interrupted mid-bang when her father decided to come home early.

That was the first time I was chased into the street buck naked, but sadly not the last. The second was when yet another girlfriend's husband unexpectedly returned from his deployment overseas—I'd had no idea she was married until a man with a gun was chasing me down the block—and the third was at an away game my rookie season in the minors. A fire alarm went off while I was in the shower. I stepped out of the bathroom to find the air already filled with smoke, panicked, and bolted without bothering to snag a towel.

Suffice it to say, I've made more than my fair share of bad calls.

But this...

I glance across the room to where Diana is unpacking a small box in the kitchen, the light catching the blond curls twisted into a bun on top of her head, and experience simultaneous twinges of elation and foreboding. The "doesn't always consider consequences" part of me is very happy to have Beach Pixie in my house, looking sexy as fuck in that nearly see-through shirt.

The practical side of me, however, knows this isn't going to end well.

I've never lived with a woman I wasn't dating or related to by blood. I know how to behave myself in those situations. I have no idea what to do with an attractive but completely off-limits roommate whose nipples I've bitten through her T-shirt.

Fuck... Even letting my thoughts drift in that direction for a split second is enough to make Long Dong Silver perk up and take notice. Which means it's time to take control of the situation before I embarrass myself.

"You want to talk house rules before the tour or after?" I dump the sponge I used to clean the carpet into the trash and cross to the sink to wash my hands.

"Why not both at once?" Diana pushes her juicer into the empty spot beside the espresso machine and turns to face me with a bright smile. "But if there are more than three, you're probably going to have to write them down and post them somewhere. I confess I have a bad head for rules."

I smile. "Why doesn't that surprise me?"

She laughs, lifting one bare, sun-kissed shoulder. "Yeah,

well, I'm not always as impulsive as I was last night. Like I said, all the romance of the evening got to me. Made me a little crazy."

"And a little smokey," I add, pointedly. "Which can't happen here, by the way. No pot or cigarettes in the house is rule number one."

Her smile fades. "Well, the cigarettes I understand completely, and I certainly wouldn't want to stink up the joint. Maybe pot could be confined to a discreet corner of the back yard?"

I shake my head. "Sorry, but this is my sister's place. She's in the Air Force and about as straight-edge as they come. She'll lose her shit if she finds out I allowed weed on the property."

Diana hums as she glances down at the counter, tracing a swirl in the marble with the tip of one finger. "Where is your sister?"

"Deployed. She accepted a short tour to Korea. She'll be there through the end of the year."

"That's a long time." Diana looks up, blinking innocently. "Some might say she would never have to know there was pot on the property, so long as the person with the pot moves out before Sis moves back in. I'm assuming you'll want me out of here before then anyway, right? Since your sister will probably want her house back."

I prop my hands on my hips, letting out a long, slow breath. "You're going to be a bad influence, aren't you?"

"No, not at all." She grins again, making me realize how feline she looks when she smiles. Like the cat who ate all the special brownies. "I promise I'll never tempt you to partake. I'll keep my habit to myself, though I will remind you that recreational marijuana is legal in Portland and used medicinally to great effect by a significant number of people nationwide. I personally use it for headaches. I used to get nasty migraines almost every day, but I'm down to one or two a month now. And I never drive or text my exes after I've been smoking so…"

"So you're basically a saint," I tease, unable to keep from flirting with her, just a little bit. Surely a little flirting never did anyone any harm.

"No," she says, her grin fading. "I'm not a saint. I'm your average, mostly confused, nearly-thirty-year-old person doing the best I can. And if we end up not getting along, I'm happy to move out. You don't even have to give me notice. Just kick me to the curb. I'm good at rolling out on the fly."

"Why would I do that?" I ask with a frown. "That would be a dick move, and I'm not a dick, Diana. I'm actually a nice guy. I promise."

"I'm sure you are," she says, in a tone that communicates she's anything but sure.

Clearly, she's had her share of bad luck with men. I think "cursed" was the word she used last night, though my memory of our conversation is whiskey-smudged. But then, I'm not really surprised. The dating pool is full of assholes and douchebags, a fact that's often made my life simpler. The jackasses of the world make it easy for a decent male human being to make a good impression on the opposite sex.

The flip side of that, of course, is that the jerks can make it harder to win a woman's trust in the first place. Once a girl's been burned by a few nasty motherfuckers, she's less inclined to let her guard down for anyone, even a guy whose intentions are honorable.

The fact that every good thing has a dark side is something I've learned the hard way.

The disorder that helps me excel at hockey—giving my in-the-moment brain something so fast-moving to focus on that I can't get distracted—is the reason I struggled with the new system when I first joined the Badgers and spent half my rookie season on the verge of getting sent back to the minors.

But thank God, that didn't happen. I adapted, my game got stronger, and my contract was renewed for another year. I've got time, one more season to prove I've got what it takes to stay in this city that feels like home, playing the game I love. If I keep my focus laser sharp, by this time next summer I could be in a position to buy my own place and put down roots.

Yet another reason to keep my focus on my game, not sexy beach pixies.

I should end this right now. I should tell Diana that she can crash here for a few weeks, until she finds another place, and start looking for a roommate with a dick, who will offer no erotic distractions.

Instead, I motion toward the patio. "Let's start the tour out back, then. Since that's where you plan to medicate."

"Sweet!" Diana heads to the French doors ahead of me. "I spend a lot of time outside, actually. I get claustrophobic if I'm cooped up for too long. Too much time spent in the woods, I guess."

"You worked for *National Geographic*?" I ask, vaguely remembering Chloe bragging about her Aunt Dee.

"Oh, I wish! That would be amazing. No, I worked for the National Park Service," she says. "Good gig, but limited advancement opportunities, so I decided it was time to move on. Now, I'm applying for jobs and working on my graphic design portfolio. Seems like most of the people looking for creative PR types around here want a background in graphics, too."

So she's currently unemployed. Which means she'll be around a lot, while I'm also around a lot during the Badgers' summer hiatus. Which means I'll have nothing to keep my mind off of my smoking-hot roomie except informal scrimmage sessions and a standing date with the gym.

I'm making plans to add in an afternoon weight training session a couple times a week, just to get out of the damned house, when we turn the corner at the back of the bungalow and Diana spins to face me, eyes glittering.

"A pool! You didn't say you had a pool!" She bounces excitedly, setting her breasts to bobbing, confirming my suspicion that she isn't wearing a bra.

I clench my jaw, fighting to keep the semi I'm sporting from becoming something more embarrassing. "Yeah. We have a pool. And pool cleaners that come by every Monday."

"That's incredible," she says, toeing off her sandals. "The only thing better than being outside is being outside and in water. Want to go swimming?"

"Right now?" I blink faster as she pulls the pencil from her bun and tosses it onto the grass, her curls cascading around her shoulders.

"Why not?" She gestures down at her tank top and shorts. "Everything I'm wearing is waterproof. I like to be ready to swim at all times, don't you?"

"I don't usually—"

A splash cuts me off as she leaps into the water, allowing her body to sink all the way to the bottom before pushing off the blue tiles and swimming to the surface with strong, smooth strokes. She breaks the water with a happy gasp that sounds a lot like the sexy sounds she was making last night when I had my thigh wedged between her legs and she was rocking against me, getting so close to coming I could taste her release on the tip of my tongue.

"Oh, this is lovely." She makes more moany orgasm sounds as she flips onto her back, effortlessly floating, her fingers and toes wiggling in the water.

But I'm not looking at her fingers and toes. I'm looking at

her chest, where her "waterproof" shirt has now become completely transparent, inspiring an instant hard-on that's impossible to fight off.

Fuuuuuuck me.

Fuck me, fuck me, fuck me…

How on earth am I supposed to resist the temptation of those beautiful tits? I need them in my hands, hot beneath my mouth as I trace each pebbled nipple in turn. I need to worship at the altar of her small but perfectly shaped breasts the way I need water and air and ample ice time every game to stave off the I'm-about-get-traded anxiety.

"Tanner?"

"Yes?" I reply, hoping I won't start drooling before I find the self-discipline to turn and walk away from the restraint-killing mermaid frolicking in my pool.

"Eyes up here?" She lifts a hand from the water to gesture to her face. "There's nothing for you below my neck, Muscle Boy. We're friends, remember?"

Utilizing more will power than I would like to admit, I force my gaze to hers. "Your shirt is pretty useless right now," I say, my voice rougher than it was before. "Just so you know."

"So? I could be naked and it wouldn't matter, right? We're friends and roommates. It's already been decided." She arches her back, causing the beautiful things I'm not supposed to look at to rise higher in the water, like two forbidden islands occupied by hostile natives. "Consider me cake, and you're on a diet."

"Cake," I echo, scowling into her golden-brown eyes.

"And I'll consider you the same." She waves a languid arm through the water, sending her spinning in a slow circle. "Though, I think I'll pretend you're nachos, if that's okay. I'm not a big fan of cake."

"That's fucked-up." I'm not talking about not being a fan

of cake, and to be sure she realizes that, I add in a take-no-prisoners tone, "Rule number two is that you keep your clothes on and wear a swimsuit in the pool."

Her expressive brows wiggle, making it clear she's irritated by the remark, but when she speaks her voice is cool. "That would be rule number one."

"What?" I'm frowning so hard at this point that my forehead is starting to hurt.

"Rule number one," she repeats. "Because I already talked you out of the old rule number one. So this is the new rule number one, which I frankly find patriarchal, condescending, and overreaching. I mean, who are you to say what I have to wear when I'm in my own home? Not my father, the last time I checked. And even my dad knows better than to tell me what to do now that I'm a fully grown woman who pays my own bills."

I'm about to snap, "It's not your home, it's my home, and there is no way I'm going to subject myself to this kind of torture on a daily basis, so please get the fuck out of the pool and go put on some not-see-through clothes," but I manage to keep my mouth shut.

If I say any of that, I'll not only be acting like the douchebag I swore I wasn't—as long as she's paying rent this is her home as much as it's mine, and only a jerk would behave otherwise—I'll also be making it obvious what she does to me. That she makes me crazy. That she transforms me into a panting, sweating, drooling man-wolf cartoon of a person, incapable of thinking clearly simply because she's beautiful and has lovely breasts that I can see through her shirt.

If I utter another word, she's got all the power, and fuck me if that's going to happen. I'm not going to become a pathetic, sex-starved, doofus in the eyes of my new roommate.

At least, not on the first day.

So with a herculean exhibition of personal fortitude, I force a smile and nod as calmly as possible considering my blood pressure is through the roof. "Fine. Suit yourself. I was just trying to help." I motion toward the eaves of the blue house visible over the fence. "Our neighbor is an old bastard who spends his free time at his window with a camera and zoom lens, but you'll probably be safe. Most perverts prefer women with more up top, right?"

A sharp bark of laughter erupts from her pink lips. "Oh no, you insulted my breast size! Whatever will I do? I guess I should crawl into a hole and cry for a few years because my body isn't curvy enough to make me a top-shelf sexual object to men who see me as a collection of female parts instead of an actual real-life person."

"I see you as an actual real-life pain in the ass," I say pleasantly. "So I'm going to head to the gym and let you finish showing yourself around. That work for you?"

"That works just fine," she snaps. "And who knows? Maybe I'll be gone before you get back."

"Suit yourself." I shrug, ignoring the voice in my head that shouts for me to apologize and make this better before I scare her away.

Let her be scared away!

It's better for everyone—Diana included. This is clearly not going to work out. The chemistry was five-alarm hot last night, yes, and I cop to finding her weirdness adorable after a few shots of whiskey. But the longer I talk to her in the harsh light of day, the more I think that I don't like this woman very much.

Right, and the raging hard-on is because you find her so fucking repulsive...

"Shut up," I mumble to the inner voice. Back in the house, I grab my keys and head for the door without bothering to change into gym clothes. I'll swing into the club store and buy something. Anything to get me out of this house even a few minutes sooner.

Hopefully, after a grueling workout, a sauna, and a cold shower, I'll be in a better frame of mind to either get to know my new roomie, or tidy up the spare room after she's removed her things.

I tell myself I don't care either way.

But I'm a dirty, rotten liar. And when I get home at eight o'clock—after three hours at the gym and another two hours shooting pool with some buddies I ran into in the parking lot—I'm absurdly pleased to hear the soft strains of the Shins emanating from her bedroom.

I hesitate in the darkened hall, hand raised to knock on her door, but after a wavering moment, I go back downstairs to take care of Wanda instead. Better to get off to a fresh start tomorrow. I'm not sure what I should say, anyway, though an apology would probably be a solid place to start.

As I harness Wanda for a walk, take her for a trot around the block, and dole out the nightly cup of pig food, I do my best to compose a good "I'm sorry, let's try the friends thing again" pitch and head to bed to feeling okay about my chances of getting off on a better foot moving forward.

But when I wake the next day, Diana is already gone and there's a note on my espresso machine—*Rule number one is fine. Sorry I was short with you. Yesterday was a crap day, and I wasn't on my best behavior. Have a good one, and I'll see you later.*

It's a perfectly pleasant note, but I can't help wishing I'd caught her before she left. I should have been the one to apologize. Or to apologize first, at least. Then maybe this fresh start would have been a warmer one.

"Warming things up is the last thing you need," I remind myself as I crumple the note in my hand.

Near my feet, Wanda grunts in agreement. I toss the note

in the trash and fetch a cup for coffee, determined to go about my business like nothing has changed.

But everything has changed, and as I pack up for another gym trip, the girl with the golden curls keeps drifting through my head, floating on the surface of my thoughts as easily as she spun through the pool water, where she remains for the rest of the day.

CHAPTER FOUR

From the texts of Amanda Esposito
and Diana Daniels

DIANA: Where have you been?
I thought today was your day off?
I've been calling you all afternoon!

AMANDA: I've been at home, waiting for you to text like a normal person. You know I hate talking on the phone.

DIANA: BUT I HAVE THINGS I NEED TO SAY IN A LOUD, ANGRY VOICE, AMANDA! TEXTING MY RAGE IS NOT NEARLY AS SATISFYING!!

AMANDA: Lol. What are you ragey about? I thought you were

enjoying the fun and exciting things the big city has to offer. Like cupcake shops, alcoholic ice cream, museums, and making out with sexy strangers on the beach.

So jealous of that last part, by the way.

There are no sexy strangers or beaches here.

It's all boring all the time.

DIANA: How many times do I have to tell you that boring is good?

Boring means nothing bad is happening to you, like having your first apartment rental fall through so you end up living with your brother's friend, who also happens to be the sexy stranger you hooked up with the night before.

AMANDA: What?! OMG you're living with Sexy Stranger?!!!

DIANA: I'm living with Sexy Stranger.

Only he's not sexy at all.

He's a bossy misogynist asshole jerk-face!

AMANDA: In his defense, you tend to think most men are misogynist asshole jerk-faces.

DIANA: That's because THEY ARE, Amanda Marie.

Have I mentioned lately how your inability to see the oppressive fist of the patriarchy is mind-boggling and frustrating beyond belief?

AMANDA: Not lately, but thanks for reminding me that I'm not completely lovable and perfect.

DIANA: Well, of course you're completely lovable and perfect. But you're also way too nice to men who do not deserve the slack you cut them.
I assume you and Wonderdick are back together already?

AMANDA: We are not back together.
We haven't talked in four days actually.

DIANA: Oh, good! Wonderful! Fantastic, even!!
Keep it up, girl! Oh, I really hope you stay broken up this time.
He's the worst.

AMANDA: I thought we were talking about your love life for once…

DIANA: Well, we aren't. Because I have no love life.
I HATE this guy. Seriously hate, Mandy.
I hate him so much I'm installing my yoga swing in the middle of his living room just to piss him off. And because it's the only place with a beam high enough, but mostly to piss him off.
Get this—yesterday he tried to make a "house rule" that I had to wear a swimsuit in the pool and then insulted the size of my chest!

AMANDA: Dare I ask why you were skinny-dipping in front of a man you barely know? I mean, aside from having made out with him for hours the night before?

DIANA: I wasn't skinny-dipping. I had on shorts and a tank top. The tank top was a tiny bit see-through when wet, it turns out, but it wasn't like I was trying to be naked. And even if I had been, where does this guy get off making fun of my itty bitties? What is this, junior high?

AMANDA: No, in junior high you didn't have breasts yet, you lucky duck.

DIANA: DO NOT START THIS AGAIN, MANDY!
I am never going to be grateful to be flat chested, and every time you try this with me, I want to stab you. Repeatedly. Preferably in one of your voluptuous Double-D-Cups.

AMANDA: And I'm never going to understand why you aren't grateful for cute, perky, manageably sized boobs! Seriously, I have a rash on my chest I can't get rid of because my boobs create their own evil, swampy, rash-inducing eco-system, Diana. And they hurt when I run unless I'm wearing enough spandex to knit a giant slingshot. And if I didn't personally know a doctor who lost a patient while she was getting a boob job, I would have them reduced in a freaking heartbeat. Half a heartbeat.

DIANA: You're out of your mind.

Amanda: Have we met, pot? I'm kettle…

Diana: Whatever. There's still no reason for a grown man to insult my chest. He's the worst. After Wonderdick. Please don't take him back, okay?

Amanda: This guy certainly picked a touchy subject, didn't he? He couldn't have aimed a better arrow if he'd known you for years.

Diana: Ugh. I'm a cliché, aren't I?
The short, flat-chested girl who is easily enraged by mention of my shortness and flat-chestedness…

Amanda: No, you're too weird to be a cliché.

Diana: Thanks.

Amanda: You're welcome.
So what's next? Are you moving out?

Diana: I can't. There isn't a single room in Portland for rent in my price range. I'm going to stick it out here for now and pray I find a job so I can start looking in the "better than the ghetto" section of Craigslist. I've got an interview at a trendy online clothing company tomorrow. They're opening their first brick and mortar store in Portland this fall and looking for someone savvy with a camera to make them look amazing on social media.

AMANDA: You'll be perfect for that! You make mushrooms and empty bird nests look like works of art. Think what you can do with actual people and cute clothes?!

DIANA: Thanks. I'm so nervous.
Nature is easy to shoot beautifully. Nature cooperates, you know?

AMANDA: I do not know. I prefer nature carefully contained, preferably surrounding a pool where I am lounging with an umbrella drink.

DIANA: How have we stayed friends for over twenty years?

AMANDA: Because I'm the only person who didn't make fun of you for being a runt in kindergarten. And because you're smart enough to recognize a keeper when you see one.

DIANA: You are a keeper, Esposito.
I wish we were gay so we could get gay-married and live happily ever after.

AMANDA: Me, too.
Even though you're a freak who likes to talk on the phone.

DIANA: I'll be calling you later, by the way. I need to hear your melodious voice telling me everything is going to be okay while I drift back and forth in my yoga swing. I think I've got it installed well enough that it won't fall out of the support beam and dump me on my ass.

AMANDA: I look forward to a text from your swing.

DIANA: Phone call.

AMANDA: Text, you monster!
Seriously, what is wrong with you?

DIANA: Love you, too. Talk later.

CHAPTER FIVE

DIANA

I hum *Sisters are Doing it for Themselves* beneath my breath as I crawl into my hot-pink yoga swing, which I have managed to install without destroying property or myself in the process.

Go, me!

I lie down and stretch into an extended corpse pose, wiggling my fingers in the air as I drift gently back and forth. In this position, the swing is like a cocoon cradling my body from head to toe. The lovely weightless yet still *supported* feeling is why I got hooked on aerial yoga. I'm not nearly as acrobatic as the rest of the ladies in my class, but the last ten minutes floating in corpse pose make up for the humiliation of being the runt with no upper body strength. And now I can enjoy a float in my own home whenever I want.

I smile like a happy worm snuggled in the dirt.

Or a happy pig burrowed deep in her nest of blankies.

Wanda really is ridiculously cute, but I'm still not on her "Acceptable Humans" list. I sweet-talked her while I dragged the ladder from the garage into the living room and drilled holes in her father's (or boyfriend's; I'm not sure how Wanda thinks of Tanner) ceiling. But Her Swineship proved immune to my usually irresistible animal-banter.

I've talked snarling pit bulls and feral cats down to the ground for a belly rub, but this pig wants no part of me.

She grunted disapprovingly the entire time I was texting with Amanda, and when I reached over to soothe her with a back rub, she started squealing like I was pulling her teeth out with a pair of needle-nosed pliers.

I quickly backed off, but she continued to whine and wail for a good fifteen minutes, making my last adjustments to the swing less than pleasant. But finally, after a few laps of her pen and some additional grumbling, Wanda got tired of complaining, rooted into her blankets, and shut her snout.

Now, the house is quiet, with nothing but the sound of the summer breeze rustling the leaves outside and the tinkle of wind chimes from the house across the street to disturb the silence. The smell of roses and lilies blooming in the front yard sweetens the air, and warm, yellow sunlight filters through gauzy, white curtains to dance on the silky fabric of my swing, making me feel like I'm wrapped in a magical pink cocoon.

It's so nice…

So very, very nice…

This bungalow is a sweet place to pass an afternoon when the man of the manor isn't in residence. With any luck, Tanner will stay at the gym pumping iron, or at the ice rink skating in circles or whatever hockey-player types do on their summer break, and we'll see very little of each other before I make my move. Surely I'll be able to find another acceptable, affordable living situation before the end of the month.

"Your dad is a dick, Wanda," I mutter, grinning when the pig oinks in response. "Sorry, but he is. You could do so much better."

A snuffle and a grunt make it clear she's not buying what I'm selling.

"Just because he's pretty to look at doesn't mean he's pretty on the inside. Trust me. I've been around the block enough to know ninety percent of men aren't worth the heartache. And even if you find one of the decent ones, he's still going to annoy the shit out of you sometimes. And when he does, you're going to want a girlfriend to bitch to, sister. I could be there for you, if you give me a chance. I'm a good listener."

Wanda doesn't respond—which I choose to believe means she's taking my counsel under advisement—and slowly the peaceful, lazy vibe of the afternoon works its magic. My tense muscles relax into the steady support of the fabric cradling my move-ravaged body, which still hasn't recovered from three weeks on Carly's lumpy couch.

I'm on the verge of drifting off into a catnap, in fact, when it happens.

One moment, I'm floating on a sea of calm; the next, my right butt cheek explodes in a supernova of pain as something sharp and merciless digs into my innocently relaxed backside with enough force to send me bolting into a seated position with a wail of agony.

"Oh my God! What the fuck?" I cry out, fighting to breathe through the waves of pain radiating from my wounded bottom flesh.

I half slide, half fall out of the swing, whimpering and hissing in distress, to discover that Wanda has escaped her enclosure.

"What did you do, pig?" I shout, but she's already scampering out of the living room, into the kitchen, and out to the backyard through a pig door I hadn't realized was there until just now.

By the time I twist my spine into the knots required to

see the torn fabric and bloodstains on my shorts that confirm that, YES, the little monster bitch pig has BITTEN ME, the beastie is cavorting in the backyard, romping and galloping through the clover to celebrate her assassination of my ass.

"No way, Wanda," I shout, voice breaking as the backs of my eyes begin to sting. "This is so not okay!"

It's not. And damn it, it *hurts*!

I grew up on a small hobby farm on Vancouver Island. At one time or another, my dad raised every kind of critter allowed by the Canadian government, and as the oldest sibling not busy playing hockey twenty-four seven, I helped out with them all. I've had horses step on my feet, been kicked in the gut by an angry sheep, and suffered many a nipped finger while feeding the baby goats.

But none of that hurt as bad as this.

Because my horse adored me, the sheep was scared of our neighbor's big brown dog that jumped the fence, and the baby goats were just babies. They all still loved me. Those injuries were accidents.

But this…

This is treachery I've done nothing to deserve, and after the stress of yesterday, I'm beginning to feel like there's a target painted on my back.

Or my ass.

Tears slip down my cheeks, and I'm gearing up for a major blubber fest when the front door opens and Tanner steps in, somehow managing to look gorgeous in a green tank top with sweat stains and a pair of slippery-looking black running shorts.

I suck in a breath, willing the tears back into my eye sockets, but it's too late. Tanner's brow is already creased with concern, and he's hurrying across the room. "What's wrong? Are you okay?"

I shake my head. "I'm fine."

He frowns, cutting a quick glance toward the hot pink swing in the middle of his otherwise very manly, very leather-and-muted-earth-tones living room before his focus returns to my no-doubt blotchy face. "Are you sure? You don't look fine."

"Yeah, well, this is just what I look like." Getting blotchy in the face if I even *think* about crying is one of my many unattractive superpowers, in addition to talking too much and too loudly and making dumb jokes when I'm nervous.

Tanner's lips part, but before he can form words, I hold up my hands and back toward the stairs, determined not to let him see what his rabid pig did to me. "It's fine, I was taking a nap in the swing and something woke me up. I'll go finish my nap in my bed and wake up looking normal in thirty or forty minutes."

"This is a swing?"

I sniff as I nod. "Yoga swing. For aerial yoga."

He scowls at the pink fabric like he expects it might be made of the skins of baby elephants. "What's it doing in the middle of the living room?"

"It's the only place it would fit. I can tie it up later so it won't be in the way." I wince as I take the first step up, the flexing of my gluteus sending a fresh wave of agony through my increasingly hot, stinging butt cheek. "I'll just have to grab the ladder out of the garage again."

"Why don't I grab it now, and we—" He breaks off, his brow smoothing as his eyes widen. "Um, uh… I think something's…happening, Diana."

Now it's my turn to frown. "What?"

He motions toward the lower half of my body, clearly doing his best not to meet my gaze. "There's, um… On your leg. I think maybe you, um…"

I glance down to see blood rolling down my thigh to drip

onto my calf, and sigh heavily, bringing my fingers to rub my eyes.

"It's not a big deal," Tanner jumps in, clearly mistaking the reason for my distress. "I mean, it's natural. Part of life. Happens to everybody. I mean, obviously not everybody, but it's nothing to be embarrassed about."

"I'm not embarrassed." My hand falls to my side with a huff.

"Seriously, I grew up the only guy in a house full of girls. I know—"

"It's not my period," I say, torn between the urge to laugh and to scream. "It's your pig. She bit me on the ass." I turn to present the evidence and Tanner curses.

"Oh shit, I'm so sorry." He turns, glancing down at Wanda's enclosure. "I'm going to have to get a better gate on the pen."

"Or you could teach the pig not to bite people," I offer dryly.

"You're right," he says, making my brows arch in surprise. "I'll call Cheyenne and tell her I'm going to have to get tough with Wanda. This is unacceptable. Chey's gone for six more months, and that's too long to live with an aggressive animal. I'll talk to the vet and do some reading, and I'll fix this. I promise."

I nod, soothed by his words. They haven't done anything to ease the pain in my rear, but it's nice that he's on my side and didn't hesitate to apologize.

"Where is she now?" he asks, scanning the room.

"She went outside to celebrate." I jab a thumb toward the kitchen. "Last time I saw her she was having a victory dance in the clover."

"A victory dance, huh?" His lips quirk as he props his hands low on his hips. "Sorry, I know it's not funny."

I shake my head. "No, it's not. But yeah…"

Our eyes meet, we smile, and for a moment I feel as connected to him as I did on the beach, when I wandered down to the water and ran into a big, sexy sweetheart who seemed to have magically appeared just when I needed him to make me forget how sad and alone I was. Tanner never felt like a stranger. He felt like someone I'd been waiting to meet, someone so familiar my brain kept insisting that we must have run into each other somewhere before.

Maybe we were friends in another life.

Sometimes I want to believe in those, on days when I think I could get this being human thing right if I had a couple hundred years and a few extra bodies to burn through while I learn from my mistakes.

"You want to head up to my bathroom?" Tanner asks softly. "I've got alcohol and gauze in the medicine cabinet. I can help patch you up."

"Patch up my butt?" I ask, lifting a brow.

His smile widens, but his gaze is still soft, vulnerable. "I figure it's the least I can do. And maybe I can treat you to ice cream after? Two scoops—one from Wanda to apologize for biting you, and one from me to apologize for being an asshole yesterday? I'm sorry for what I said by the pool. I was out of line."

I cross my arms and then immediately uncross them, not wanting him to realize I'm self-conscious, or that his sweet side makes me fluttery in a way I haven't felt in a long time. "Well, thank you. I accept your apology."

"I'm glad." He cocks his head and a damp lock of hair slips onto his forehead, making it impossible not to notice how sexy he looks all sweaty. "And what about ice cream? There's a place a few blocks over, close enough to ride bikes if you want. I can lower the seat on Chey's for you. I was going to offer it to you, anyway, since it doesn't seem like you have a car."

"No, I don't have a car." I bristle, even though everything he's said is very nice and completely generous. "But I think riding a bike would be painful at the moment."

He winces. "Right. Sorry. Let's get your bite cleaned and dressed and I can drive us over. Though I should probably take a quick shower first so I don't stink up the joint." He grins gamely as he ambles across the room. The hair on the back of my neck lifts in protest, insisting we want no part of that grin or fluttery feelings or anything else this dangerous person is offering.

Dangerous and manipulative, I realize, eyes narrowing.

"Are you using your devil pig's bad behavior to trick me into going out with you?" I ask, holding my ground on the second step as he stops at the bottom of the stairs.

He blinks, some of the warmth fading from his eyes. "No, I'm trying to be friendly and apologize."

"Because I was serious," I say firmly. "I'm not going to date you, Tanner. Niceness and ice cream won't change that."

"I get it," he says, jaw muscles flexing as he nods.

"And I'm not up for meaningless sex, either," I add, unable to stop my stupid mouth from running. "So if you think that bandaging my butt is going to turn into something more, you can put that idea away right now. In fact, it's probably better if I do it myself."

"Why? Because if I get one look at your bare ass cheek, I'll turn into a wild animal incapable of controlling myself?" He snorts. "You have a pretty high opinion of yourself, don't you, Squirt?"

"Don't call me that," I snap. "And no, I don't. I just happen to live in the real world where I know letting a guy who's got a hard-on for me fondle my bare ass is probably a bad idea."

"A hard-on for you?" He laughs, a rough sound wrenched from his throat. "Don't worry, sweetheart. That hard-on lasted about as long as it took for me to realize you're a lot less fun when you're sober."

My jaw drops, but I force an angry laugh of my own. "Ditto, buddy. And nice to know my gut take on you yesterday wasn't wrong." I cross my arms, cocking my head in mock curiosity. "Was it hard for you? Keeping your asshole side under wraps for five minutes?"

"You're the one who's acting like I'm about to sexually assault you when all I'm trying to do is help and apologize!"

My glare intensifies. "No, I am not acting like you're about to assault me. If I were, you would be on the floor right now, Muscle Boy. I might be small, but I know how to defend myself."

"Jesus Christ, Diana." He lifts his eyes and his clawed hands toward the ceiling, as if praying for divine intervention. "How did asking to buy you ice cream turn into you threatening to beat me up?"

"I'm going to my room." I stand up straighter, refusing to show weakness. I'm not sure how we got here, either, only that Muscle Boy and I are like ingredients in an unpredictable science experiment—throw us together and dramatic things tend to happen. "I will borrow some first aid supplies from your medicine cabinet on the way, if that's acceptable."

He sighs heavily as his eyes slide closed. "Yes. It's acceptable. Knock yourself out."

"Thank you," I offer primly as I turn to climb the steps.

"You're welcome. And I'll take this swing down for you, too."

"Fine. And I'll put it back up tomorrow. And drill another hole in your support beam while I'm at it."

He curses again.

For a moment, I consider telling him that before I move out I plan to patch the hole so perfectly he'll never know it was there, but then I decide that since *I'm* the one bleeding from my ass because of his stupid pig, I'll let him be pissed off. He can sit and spin for all I care. I can't believe I thought he had a sweet side, or that I let it make me fluttery.

As soon as I doctor my butt and do some Googling to ensure I'm not going to catch a deadly infection from a pig bite, I'm going to troll Craigslist for a new living situation. Or maybe I'll troll for a car instead.

I could live in the car and use it to drive to my fantastic new job I'm going to land any day now. I can pull that off. It's summer, and the weather is sleeping-in-your-car friendly. And it will be an adventure, like the time I hiked halfway across Ireland with Amanda because she was too scared to get into the car with almost everyone who pulled over to offer us a ride.

I consider calling Mandy to tell her how horrible Tanner is, but she probably wouldn't pick up, and then I would have to leave a message. And I hate leaving messages.

Answering machines make me feel lonely, like I've reached out to take someone's hand only to have them turn and walk away, making it clear how pathetic and unlovable I am.

My best friend has a phone phobia, and I have a message phobia. We're opposites in just about every way, but we've been like sisters since we were kids.

People don't have to have a lot in common in order to get along, and I get along with almost everyone. I'm an outgoing person and I make friends easily. Tanner and I should be able to make this work. We certainly got along fine before we lived under the same roof.

Maybe if I apologize for accusing him of having a hard-on for me, and promise to keep things purely friendly from now on, we could have a fresh start. It would be nice not to have to live in a car or in a hovel or in my brother's guest room, where I'll be exposed to so much love and happiness there will be little to no chance of not spiraling into a deep, jealousy-inspired depression.

I'm about done sticking gauze to my injured cheek with tape and seriously considering an apology when I hear Tanner outside, talking in a cozy, affectionate voice. I cross to the window and look down to see him out in the yard, tossing a red ball across the grass, and Wanda running for it as fast as her pudgy legs can carry her.

In seconds, she's got the ball in her mouth and gallops back to Tanner, who greets her with a "Good girl! What a good girl, Wanda. Such a good pig."

I scowl, glaring at the jerkface and his evil spirit animal with enough intensity to set him on fire.

He's *praising* the pig.

He's praising and *playing fetch* with the pig that just ripped a hole in my backside.

All thoughts of apologizing exit the thought-building, and my head is immediately filled with ways to get revenge on both master and swine. I'm rarely a vengeful person, but when I am…

Postponing the Google search on death by pig bite infection, I call Justin, another hockey weirdo and my brother's best friend.

Unlike Mandy, he picks up on the second ring.

"What's up, Little Dee?" he asks. He is one of the few people who can call me "little" and not make it sound like an insult to my hypersensitive ears.

"I need dirt on Nowicki, my new roommate," I say softly. "Whatever I can use to make him squirm."

"Is he misbehaving with you?" Justin's tone goes from light to deep and dangerous in a heartbeat. "If so, you don't need dirt, sweetheart. I'll be over there in ten minutes and his face and my fist will have a nice long talk."

"No, it's nothing like that," I say, experiencing a flash of guilt. Yes, Tanner is a jerk, but I don't want to get him in the doghouse with a senior member of his team. And Justin, as sweet and goofy as he is, can be even more of a papa bear than my brother when he thinks someone he cares about isn't being treated well.

"It's just a difference of opinion about where my yoga swing should go in the house," I add, improvising. "But it's nothing that can't be solved by an attitude adjustment and some creative bargaining."

Justin laughs, a wicked, relish-filled chuckle. "Well, in that case, I'm you're man, girl. I've got dirt on the Wickster for days. We were engaged in a brief but brutal prank war a few months back. I didn't make him cry, but I got really, really close."

I click my pen, grinning as I position it over my yellow pad, gaze still fixed out the window to where Tanner and Wanda are celebrating their victory.

Too bad that victory is going to be short-lived…

"Give it to me, Cruise. I'm ready."

CHAPTER SIX

TANNER

*B*reakout drills are important. They're not as fun as shooting drills or breakaway drills, but sometimes the puck ends up behind the fucking net, and you have to get it out from behind the fucking net, and so you practice.

You drill.

I accepted this fact a long time ago, but that doesn't make it any easier to focus today. Not when I'm sleep deprived, sanity deprived, and tormented by the ghosts of the filthy dreams I had about my captain's little sister last night.

Thankfully, Brendan doesn't seem to be a mind reader. He's even more laid back than usual, practically humming with affability as he slaps the puck behind the net to start the drill.

Petrov retrieves the puck and skates it up the ice, moving fast. I take my position for the outlet pass, but suddenly Adams is there, circling me like a rabid shark, fast and furious and annoying as fuck. I adjust my position to get my stick open and Petrov, as always, makes a perfect tape-to-tape pass. But Adams is quick to pounce. He's an aggressive little bastard, but there are dangers associated with coming in hard.

All I have to do is chip the puck up the boards around him, and I'm off to the races. In my peripheral vision, I spot Petrov in support position and prepare to make my move. But instead of going where I tell it to go—where I have very clearly guided it with my stick—the puck ends up in Adams' skates.

Adams dances over it, takes control, and slaps the disc into our open net.

I curse, Adams laughs, and Petrov swoops back across the ice like a large, dark, disappointed bird of prey that's been denied his kill.

"Try to make him work for it next time, Nowicki," Brendan shouts, amusement in his voice. "Next group!"

I head back to the bench, cursing sleep deprivation and misbehaving pucks.

"You okay?" Petrov drops onto the bench beside me, still breathing hard but not as hard as I am, making me wonder how much cardio he does every day. He's five years older than I am and carrying at least thirty extra pounds, but he sure as hell doesn't move like it.

"Fine. Just didn't sleep for shit last night." I stretch my neck to one side, keeping my focus on the ice as Brendan skates by, cruising into position for the next set of drills.

When I was invited to join my captain and a few of his friends from the team for informal summer skates to help keep my skills sharp during the break, I was flattered. Now, I wish I'd failed whatever test made me scrimmage material and trustworthy enough to cohabitate with Brendan's sister.

I'm never going to survive living with Diana Daniels. We're either going to kill each other or Brendan is going to kill me when he realizes I've got a hard-on for his sister that won't quit.

I spent the entire night tossing and turning, hyperaware of the infuriating sex kitten down the hall, dividing my sleepless hours between replaying every moment of our make-out session on the beach and imagining all the filthy things we could get up to in that yoga swing. If it even has anything to do with yoga, which I doubt. Installing a sex swing in my living room that she intends to use with someone else simply to torture me seems like the sort of thing that the devil in hot woman form would find amusing.

"What do you know about aerial yoga?" I ask Petrov as our second group of three launches in the breakout drill and Brendan shouts coachy things from the other side of the ice.

Petrov gives one of his Russian shrugs, the ones that could mean "everything" or "absolutely nothing." I never know unless he speaks. Petrov was born in this country, but he's got a hint of an accent and an Eastern European caginess about him. Suffice it to say, I wouldn't be surprised to find he's a secret agent for one side or the other.

"It's like stretching with circus tricks," he says, pointing to the rink's ceiling. "They hang fabric from the ceiling and then do flips in it. My ex was into it for a few months last summer, but she ended up with bruises on her arms from getting the tension wrong, so she quit. Said she didn't want the people where she worked to think I beat her."

I grunt. "That's a nice conclusion to jump to."

Another Russian shrug. "I'm a big, scary-looking guy who has a rep for losing my temper on the ice. I get it."

"Why did you and Eva break up, anyway?" I ask, trying not to think about Diana doing sexy circus tricks in that hot-pink swing. "I thought things were good with you two."

"She wants kids someday. It got to the point where we had to start taking stuff like that seriously, so we did. And we broke up." He tips his water bottle up, squeezing a stream into his open mouth. I figure that's the end of it, but then he adds, "That's the last time I put that discussion off until five months in. Next time, I'm laying it out there on the first date. No sense in getting involved with someone who wants things I'm never going to be able to give her."

I'm tempted to ask why he's anti-kid, but keep my mouth shut, instead. It took me a few years to adjust to being surrounded by other men instead of a family of women, but I've learned to take it easy with the personal questions. If Petrov wants to talk about why he doesn't want kids—or maybe can't have kids—he will.

But he probably won't. Petrov keeps his cards so close to his chest I'm not sure he's even playing the game.

"So, I heard you let Daniels' sister move in with you," he says, surprising me. I hadn't realized the news was getting around. "How's that working out?"

I let out a long, slow sigh and am surprised again by the soft rumble of Petrov's laughter.

"I figured. I've met Diana," he says with a smile. "She's a firecracker."

"That's one word for it," I grumble.

He laughs again before nudging me with his elbow and adding in a softer voice, "Just be careful. It's not a good idea to get involved with someone with close ties to the team. Brendan's one of the most solid guys I know, but he'll still make your life fucking miserable if you put your hands on his sister."

"No danger of that." I snort. "She hates my guts. And I'm not too fond of her, either, honestly."

Petrov shifts on the bench, studying me through narrowed eyes, like a surgeon deciding where to make the first incision.

"What?" I finally ask, because there's only so much of the Russian stare I can take before my scalp starts to itch.

"There's a thin line between hate and fucking like

rabbits," Petrov says, tossing his water bottle back into his bag. "A very thin one."

"No way, man," I huff. "She's made it clear she's not interested. Not even a little bit."

Except when we were making out like horny teenagers and she said she would want a lot more than kissing if she went back to my room with me…

Petrov's frown becomes a full-blown scowl, as if he's read my mind and found the thoughts there less than comforting. "She needs to find a new place to live. Yesterday. You can crash at my place until she's out if you need to. The pool house is empty."

"Thanks, but it's going to be fine. I doubt Diana will stick around much longer. She has a job interview today. Once she's got a steady gig, she'll be out as soon as she can throw her shit back in her bags. Not only does she hate me, but she and Wanda are pretty much sworn enemies."

Petrov grunts. "Where I come from, pigs are for eating."

"It's my sister's," I say defensively. "She's serving her country. The least I can do is take care of her pig until she gets home."

"Well, if you change your mind, I have experience curing meat." He stands, preparing to head back onto the ice for the final scrimmage. "You could welcome your sister home with prosciutto and applewood smoked bacon."

I shudder, making the bastard laugh again.

"You're going soft, rookie," he says. "You've fallen in love with a pig."

"I have not fallen in love with a pig," I protest, but the truth is that hearing Petrov talk about turning Wanda into bacon has soured my stomach.

I can't eat an animal I've taken for walks, let alone one smart enough to figure out how to pop the lock on her gate, obey fifteen different verbal commands (when she's in the mood), and hold a grudge against my new roomie—because even Wanda can sense that Diana and I are not "just friends" material.

Back on the ice, we line up for a two on one drill. I'm one of the attacking players who will be doing my damnedest to score against Saunders and Wallace, who's playing goalie. Petrov starts the drill, carrying the puck up the ice. I get to an open spot near the boards and he throws a beautiful saucer pass that spirals through the air, past Saunders, to land right in front of me. I cradle the puck with my stick and head for the goal. Petrov, anticipating the play, skids into position for a back-door tap in.

I move in hard, prepping for the pass, Saunders hot on my heels. But I'm ahead of him. I've got this, there's no doubt in my mind.

I'm a split second from slapping the puck to Petrov when I feel something hard jamming into my armpit. I realize it's Saunders hooking me with his damn stick, and then suddenly I'm off balance, scrambling to get my skates under control before I land flat on my back.

By the time I recover, the puck has glided harmlessly away toward Wallace, who slaps it into the corner.

"Do you have eyes today Nowicki?" Brendan shouts from center ice.

I spin, jabbing a finger at Saunders. "That was a dirty play. He hooked me!"

"If you hadn't been holding on to the puck like it was your baby, he wouldn't have had the chance to hook you," Brendan says. "Plus, dirty shit happens, and the benefit of the doubt on penalties rarely falls to the rookie. You have to be ready for more experienced players to take advantage, and play through it. That's just the way it is."

"Fuck the way it is." I tap my stick hard on the ice in front of me. "A fucking penalty is a fucking penalty."

"Well, sorry to break it to you, but life ain't fair." Brendan frowns, cocking his head. "What's up with you today? Everything all right at home?"

The words send a cold rush of anxiety sweeping through me, taking the edge off my anger. Fuck, does he know? Has Diana said something about what a shitty roommate I'm proving to be? Is that why he's riding my ass and letting Saunders get away with being a shit?

And if so, how much more irritated will he be if he learns that I've already made out with his sister and devoted far too many hours to fantasizing about all the wicked, wonderful things I would like to do to Diana if we could stop hating each other for more than ten minutes.

I clear my throat. "No. Just woke up on the wrong side of the bed this morning, I guess."

Brendan's eyes narrow, but after a moment he nods. "All right. Take a lap and we'll try it again."

I push off, gliding around the net on the opposite side of the ice, promising myself that I'll make this right before it's too late. I'm not sure how to pull it off just yet, but there's no question about it now. Diana has to go. She has to go somewhere far, far away, before we cross that thin line from hate to fucking like bunnies and I end up setting off a dirty bomb in the middle of my career, one year into my first NHL contract.

CHAPTER SEVEN

TANNER

I take my time on the bike ride home from downtown, brainstorming exit strategies. The easiest option would be to tell Diana that I'll stay with Petrov for a couple of weeks while she finds a new living situation.

But there's no way Petrov will put up with me bringing Wanda along for the visit. And if I leave Diana and Wanda alone, one or both of them will end up dead, and I don't want that on my conscience.

I could bundle Wanda into the car and take her to Santa Barbara to visit my mom and stepdad, but the pig requires more travel bags than my other sister's two kids, and I'm not up for extended family bonding time right now. My mom is psychic when it comes to the emotional state of her offspring. The second I set foot in the house, she'll be able to tell that I'm lonely and worried about how my second season as a Badger is going to pan out.

If Diana sticks around, it's going to pan out like a batch of shit brownies. You were a fucking mess on the ice today, and it's all that woman's fault.

It's not *all* her fault—it takes two to whip up a steaming

hot, suffocating, focus-shattering batch of sexual tension—but I know myself too well to think the way I feel about Diana is going to change. Yes, I may shift back and forth from finding her amusing to infuriating, but I'm always going to want to get her naked and make her moan. Whether she's being silly and charming or a sarcastic pain in my ass, she's sexy as fuck.

She's even sexy when she's crying, I realize as I glide into the driveway to find Diana sitting on the porch steps with red eyes, blotchy cheeks, and a tissue balled into a wad in her fist.

I grit my teeth, praying Wanda hasn't attacked again before I've figured out how to implement the behavior corrections I read about last night. Yes, I need to get Diana out of the house, but I don't want her to be scared away by the threat of repeated pig violence.

"What's up?" I swing off my bike, letting it fall to the grass in the front yard.

She glances up, her eyes widening, and turns as if to stand…only to sag back onto the top step a moment later. "Sorry. I would have gone to my room to cry, but Wanda's out of her pen again and I didn't feel like being chased by a bottom-chomping goblin. I barely made it out of the house this morning without getting attacked, and that was when I was young and full of hope."

"I'll put her in the backyard and disable the pig door right now," I say. "And I'm going to get the aggression under control, I promise. I did some reading last night on the mini pig sites and got some good advice."

Diana nods, swiping the tears from her cheeks with her soggy tissue. "Sounds good. Thank you.

I start toward the gate leading to the backyard, but stop before I've made it off the walk.

If Wanda isn't the reason she's crying, then…

Don't ask. It's none of your business, and you don't care anyway. It's not like you're friends.

No, we're not friends. But I do care. I don't like seeing her cry.

"So why aren't you young and hopeful anymore?" I ask, telling myself I'll head straight for the backyard if she offers a smartass response.

Instead, she sniffs and her shoulders curl forward. "The job interview."

"Bad?" I take a tentative step forward.

"Yeah. Really bad." She props her elbows on her knees and drops her chin into her hands with another sniff. "They laughed at me. In the mean-girl way."

I frown. "Why would they do that?"

"Because they run a trendy clothing store and I wore a sundress I bought five years ago to the interview," she says, drawing my attention to the soft-looking yellow-checked dress she's wearing. "And I wasn't wearing enough makeup. Or the right shoes."

"You don't need makeup," I say gruffly, wishing I could give the jerks who made her cry a piece of my mind. "And what the hell do shoes have to do with whether you take good pictures?"

She looks up at me, eyes shining. "Nothing. And I normally wouldn't care what a bunch of superficial jerks thought of me, but I needed that job. And they didn't even look at my resume or portfolio." Her eyes roll skyward. "I mean, they looked, but I could tell they weren't *seeing* it, you know? They were seeing that I was a fashion disaster with scuffed sandals who doesn't moisturize enough."

She sucks in a breath, her bottom lip trembling. "One of them gave me lotion samples on the way out because 'women in their thirties need to take moisturizing seriously,' but..." Her features crumple as she finishes in a pitiful wail, "But I'm only twenty-seven and I'm too poor to afford fancy lotions and creams!"

I sit down next to her, putting my arm around her shoulders and pulling her in for a hug. "Hey, don't cry. Forget those bitches. You would have hated working for them anyway. You'll find something way better. I know you will."

She leans into me, not seeming to mind that I'm sweaty and gross from practice and the bike ride home. "But what if I don't? What if I should have stayed in the woods with the animals and trees and other things that aren't disgusted by my hideous, old-before-my-time face, oversize pores, and lack of fashion sense?"

I laugh. I can't help it.

She looks up at me, her expression so stricken that I hurry to assure her, "I'm laughing because that's ridiculous. Your face is beautiful. You're beautiful. Those women were probably just jealous."

"No, they weren't," she sniffs.

"Yes, they were. When I first met you, I thought you were a teenager you look so young. The last thing you have to worry about is being old before your time, or needing a bunch of expensive creams."

She swipes at her cheeks, but I can feel the tension beginning to seep from her muscles. "That's because it was dark. And you're a dude. Dudes are bad at guessing how old women are."

I make a noncommittal sound.

"But I like that you asked how old I was," she adds in a softer voice. "That you wanted to make sure I was old enough to roll around with on the sand. That was sweet. And classy."

"I'm a sweet, classy guy." I rub my palm gently up and down her bare arm. "When I'm not being the guy you like to fight with, of course."

She shifts away, but not too far away, and looks up, meeting my gaze. "I don't like to fight. Honestly, I don't."

I study her eyes, amazed at how soft and warm they are when she's not pissed at me. "Me, either. I hate it, actually. I don't like seeing people upset, let alone when I know I'm the one who's pissing them off."

"You're a people pleaser," she observes, her eyebrows doing that rippling thing they do when she's thinking.

"I guess so," I admit. "I just want to be the nice guy. For a long time after my dad bailed, it was just me, my two older sisters, and my mom. I got an up close and personal look at what assholes do to the women in their lives. Way before I was old enough to date, I knew I didn't want to be one of them."

Diana cocks her head. "So why aren't you living happily ever after, Tanner Nowicki? As a real life sweetheart with a sexy job and a body that won't quit, I would think you would have met Miss Right by now. Is it Wanda cramping your style, or do you have creepy secret habits I haven't observed yet?"

"I don't think I have any creepy habits." I shrug uncomfortably, trying not to think too much about the nice things she said. Just because she thinks I have a body that won't quit doesn't mean she wants to do anything more than sit next to that body on the porch. "My last relationship was on the rocks when I got drafted. We broke up before I moved, and since I've been in Portland I've been too focused on the game to date much."

Her brow furrows. "Do you find your job stressful? I imagine it would be. I mean, Brendan never acts stressed, not about hockey, anyway, but he's a weirdo."

I smile. "In what way?"

"He's so chill. Always has been. Even when he was a newborn. My parents said he hardly ever cried." She sniffs and a spark of her usual mischief flashes in her eyes. "So they were completely unprepared for me."

"Bad baby?"

"The worst, according to the stories. But since I can't remember any of that, I prefer to believe my parents' claims of colic screams at all hours of the day and night are exaggerated." She nudges my knee with hers. "What about you?"

"Good baby. Though, allegedly, I liked to eat a lot."

Diana smiles, one of those sunny grins that brings out the gold flecks in her brown eyes. "No, I meant the game. Does being in the NHL stress you out?"

"Not really. Not most of the time, anyway. Hockey's always been the one thing I'm really good at. But I had a rough start to the season last year." I roll my shoulders, the memories of those first few weeks enough to make my muscles ball up in stress knots. "It got better, but if I want to stay with the Badgers, I've got to bring it from game one this season. No backsliding or spacing out."

She's quiet for a long time, but I can tell her wheels are spinning. Her eyes are searching my face, and her brows are arching and bending in ways I didn't know eyebrows could arch and bend.

Finally, I can't help but laugh.

"What?" she asks, blinking.

I shake my head. "Nothing. I just…" I trace one of her pale brows with my finger, an intimacy she allows, making my voice huskier as I add, "You do funny things with your eyebrows."

Her lips quirk into a smile that's a little shy and completely adorable. "I know. I can't help it. That's where my thoughts go."

"I like it. And you look like sunshine in this dress. I would have hired you in a heartbeat, just to have you around to brighten up the joint."

She swallows, her grin fading.

"What's wrong?" I wait for her to tell me I've overstepped my bounds again and tripped her "Someone's Trying to Pick Me Up" radar.

"Nothing." She bites her bottom lip. "Actually, there is something. Can I ask a favor?"

I nod. "Sure."

"Can you to take Wanda outside and stay out there for ten or fifteen minutes?"

Now it's my turn to blink. "Why's that?"

"I may have done something…" Her eyebrows telegraph guilt as her gaze slides to the right, lingering on the rosebushes.

"Done something," I echo. "Something like what?"

"Something to get revenge that I'm regretting right now…"

I withdraw my arm from around her shoulders. "Revenge for what?"

"For Wanda biting me and you taking her out to play fetch afterward like she isn't a witch in need of an attitude adjustment," Diana says, lifting her hands into the air in surrender. "But like I said, I regret it now. And I don't want to get in a fight after you've been so nice. I mean, in my opinion what I did isn't that big a deal, but Justin told me this particular thing really gets under your skin, so…"

My gaze narrows at Cruise's name, and the hairs rise on the back of my neck. "Justin gave you prank advice?"

She nods, nose wrinkling. "Sorry."

"Show me." I stand, reaching a hand down to her, curling my fingers in a beckoning motion when she hesitates. "Come on. I won't be mad. I just want to see."

She shakes her head. "No, you don't. You really don't."

"I need to see," I insist. "If I'm going to teach Justin a

lesson about spreading stories outside the locker room, I need to make sure the punishment fits the crime."

Diana stands, fingers tangling nervously together in front of her. "Oh no, please don't. Let me run upstairs and fix this, and then forget I said anything, okay? I don't want to be the reason you and Justin start prank-warring again. That's not going to help you stay focused and at the top of your game when the season starts."

I start toward the front door, but Diana stops me, grabbing my elbow with both hands and holding on with surprising strength.

"Do not go upstairs," she says, eyes wide.

"I'm going upstairs."

She shifts in front of me, so close her sandals are on the toes of my tennis shoes. "No, Tanner. You can't. I won't let you."

"And how are you going to stop me, Squirt?" I ask, keenly aware of her strawberry-and-soap scent and how much I would like to kiss that stubborn mouth of hers.

"Call me that again and you're going to regret it." She lifts her chin, bringing her lips closer to mine.

"Is that right?"

"Yes, it is." Her voice drops to a whisper as she sways closer still, until her breasts are mere inches from my chest.

I hold her gaze as the air between us grows thick, loaded with dangerous possibilities. "I don't think so, Daniels. I think you're all talk and no action."

"The mannequins I put in your bed would indicate otherwise," she says, her breath catching as I slip my arm around her waist, drawing her against me.

"You put mannequins in my bed?"

She nods, lids drooping to half-mast as her focus shifts from my eyes to my mouth and lingers there. "I did. How does that make you feel?"

"Repulsed," I say, loving the soft sigh that escapes her lips as my hand slips down to squeeze the uninjured side of her ass through the thin cotton of her dress. "I may never sleep in my bed again."

"I'm sorry."

"No, you're not," I shoot back, well aware that most people think my irrational fear of mannequins is hilarious.

"I am. I swear." Her arms drift around my neck, where her fingers thread into my still-damp hair.

"I'm sweaty," I warn, backing her toward the door.

"I don't care," she says.

"You like me dirty?" I pin her against the warm wood, my arms on either side of her up-turned face.

"I do." Her nails dig lightly into my neck. "I'd like to get you even dirtier, if that's okay with you."

"Might be hard to do if everything below your neck is still off-limits." I catch the strap of her sundress, running my finger beneath it, desperate for a taste of her sun-warmed skin. "I thought you were cake and I was on a diet?"

"It's okay to cheat on a diet every now and then, though, right?" Her breath comes faster as I cup her breast through the soft cotton of her dress, deliberately avoiding the tight nipple beading beneath the fabric. "As long as you go back to making healthy choices after?"

Healthy choices...

There is nothing healthy about this. Fucking my captain's sister is a serious breach of the Badger code and a good way to end up on the shit list of every guy on the team. But even if there were no bro code violation on the line, getting naked with my roommate—a woman I'll have to run into every day between now and whenever she finds another place to live—is plain stupid, especially considering what I know about this woman so far.

Diana doesn't want a relationship or even a steady fuck

buddy. She wants to get dirty with me and then go back to treating me like a temptation best avoided.

As much as I would like to get that tight nipple in my mouth and Diana on top of me, riding my cock until she comes screaming my name, this is a bad idea. So even though I'm as hard as a goal pipe, I force my hand from her breast and step back with a shake of my head. "I don't want to be a cheat meal. That's not my style."

Her lashes flutter and her breath rushes out. "What?"

"I don't do one-night stands or one-afternoon stands or whatever this would be." I motion between us before crossing my arms at my chest, the better to keep my traitorous hands from reaching for her again.

"You're turning down casual, no-strings-attached sex?" she asks, brow furrowing. "Are you for real?"

I incline my head. "I am."

She huffs. "You realize any other man on the planet would be high-fiving himself and tripping over his pants because he couldn't get his dick out of them fast enough. You get that, right?"

I stand up straighter. "You've got a low opinion of men."

"I have an *accurate* opinion of men," she says, a wounded note creeping into her voice. "But whatever. Fine. I won't bother you again."

"You aren't—"

"No, it's fine. Really," she cuts me off, fumbling for the door handle. "I'll be in my room. Let me know if you need help with the mannequins. Sorry again about that."

She retreats inside, dashing across the living room toward the steps so quickly that by the time I close the door behind me, she's already out of sight.

I run a clawed hand through my hair with a sigh.

Sometimes I wish I were like those men Diana was talking about—guys who can separate sex and feelings and fuck a woman they're attracted to without getting attached. But I'm not, and despite what my dick has to say about it, this is for the best.

For the best, for the best, for the best...

I repeat the mantra as I scan the living room for Wanda, finding nothing but an empty enclosure and a pile of pink blankets in front of the television, where she likes to watch Good Morning America. Figuring she must be out in the backyard, I start for the stairs, intending to make my way swiftly past Diana's room and into my own, where I will ignore the mannequins until I've had a long, cold, hard-on softening shower.

I seriously have no plan to pause at Diana's door, let alone intrude on her privacy.

But then she screams—a high-pitched howl of terror that shatters the silence of the sleepy summer afternoon—and I act without thinking. Before I realize I've turned the doorknob, I'm inside her room, running around the bed as Diana streaks out of the bathroom with Wanda hot on her heels.

I have a split second to realize that Diana is naked—every toned, sun-kissed inch of her bare, save for the few inches covered by the washcloth she's clutched to her chest—and then she's in my arms.

I lift her into the air, out of reach of my poorly behaved piglet.

"She was hiding behind the door," Diana squeals, clinging to my neck. "She was hiding there, waiting for me! And then she jumped out, snapping her teeth like something out of a fucking nightmare!"

"Bad pig. Very bad pig!" I shout, the unusually loud scolding sending Wanda scampering across the carpet and out the door, wailing like she's the one who was ambushed on her way to the shower.

"Close the door," Diana gasps. "Oh please, hurry. Close the door before she can get back in."

I cross the room, Dee still clinging to my neck, and kick the door closed.

Only then, when we are well and truly alone, do I glance down at the very naked, very beautiful, very sexy woman in my arms.

Our eyes meet, awareness burns hot and fierce in air between us, and my last gasp of willpower evaporates in a puff of steam.

And apparently the self-control-defeating disease is catching…

"Fine, let's do this, Muscle Boy," Diana says.

A moment later, my mouth is devouring hers and I'm aiming us both for her bed.

CHAPTER EIGHT

DIANA

You can't do this! You can't! You have to stop! Now!

A hundred exclamatory sentences sound off between my ears, but the only things coming out of my mouth are sighs and moans and gasps as Tanner tosses me on the bed and strips off his shirt, revealing the most beautiful torso I've ever seen. There are muscles—so many delicious muscle-y muscles—but it's the elegant, streamlined arrangement of the muscles as they ripple from his broad shoulders down to his narrow waist that takes my breath away.

He's a work of art, a thing of beauty I would feel compelled to photograph immediately if I weren't so desperate to touch him, taste him, and feel his skin hot and hungry against mine.

"I want to memorize your chest with my tongue," I murmur in a lust-fogged voice.

"I want to memorize your pussy with mine," he responds, sending electricity zapping between my legs.

"Oh, yes, that sounds good." I moan as he stretches

himself out on top of me, nudging my thighs apart in a proprietary way that's sexy as hell. And then he lowers his hips, pressing his erection against me through his shorts as he whispers "Guess I lied about that hard-on," into my ear, and I'm gone.

All the pent up sexual frustration of the past eight months comes roaring to the surface. I'm like a juice-faster thrown into a room full of steak and donuts—ravenous to the point of violence.

I dig my nails into Tanner's shoulders and ravage his mouth with mine until my breath is coming fast and my blood is pounding in my ears and every inch of my skin is screaming to get closer, closer, until that thick, delicious cock is buried between my legs. I want to be fucked hard and fast and deep, to be taken with a ferocity that assures me I'm going to get what I need, what I've been deprived of, what I'm so desperate for that when Tanner tries to kiss his way south toward my breasts and regions beyond, I grab a handful of his hair and hold on tight.

"Fuck me first." I catch the top of his shorts with my toes and shove them clumsily down his strong thighs. "Fuck me first. Other stuff later."

"Are you always this bossy in bed?" he asks, even as he helpfully assists in disposing of his shorts, eliminating the barrier between his cock and my fingers.

I reach down, capturing the burning length in my hand and stroking him up and down, drawing a groan from low in his throat. "Not always, but when I am it's because I'm desperate and not to be trifled with. I need you, Tanner. Inside me. Right now. Right fucking now."

"Wait." His breath rushes over my lips as I stroke him again, harder this time, summoning another hungry sound from his lips.

"No waiting. No more waiting." I fit the head of his cock to where I'm wet, aching, pulsing with a need that's dizzying in its intensity.

I'm beyond thinking rationally, beyond thinking about anything except getting Tanner buried inside me ASA-fucking-P and filling the ravenous emptiness gnawing away at my core.

I don't hear the doorbell ring. I don't hear anyone call out.

I only become aware that something isn't right when Tanner pins my arms forcefully to the mattress above me and whisper-shouts, "Your brother! Coming up the stairs! Right now! You have to get dressed."

And then he's gone, rolling off of me so fast the rush of cool air makes me flinch.

I sit up, determined to get my hands on Tanner and pull him back on top of me, when I hear footsteps on the stairs and a familiar voice saying, "Diana? Are you up here? I got your text."

My text?

I have no idea what he's talking about. But I know Brendan will be traumatized if he walks in on me naked, and that trauma will swiftly transform into purple-faced rage if he sees Tanner scrambling into his clothes at the foot of my bed. Yes, Brendan has always respected my ability to choose my own sexual adventures, but he's also my brother, a big fan of rules, and not one to find it cute that his teammate is banging his sister a day after we moved in together.

"Just a second!" I call out. "Be right down."

"I'm already up here," Brendan says from right outside my fucking door. "Can I come in?"

"No!" I shout as Tanner drops to the floor in a push-up position, hiding behind the bed. "No, you can't! I'm naked! I was napping naked and I just woke up."

"All right, relax," he says, his voice already moving away from the door. "I'll meet you downstairs. Though I'm not sure that pig likes me, either. She tried to trip me on the way up the stairs."

"Good girl, Wanda," Tanner whispers, sending an unexpected giggle bubbling up my throat.

I smash a fist to my lips, refusing to incriminate myself. After a beat, I regain control and call, "Take a seat on the porch outside. She can't get to you there, and I'll be out in just a sec."

I wait until my brother's footsteps retreat and the front door slams shut before turning back to Tanner, who is now lying on the floor wearing nothing but his shorts and a ravenous expression. He looks like he wants to push me back onto the bed and fuck me until I scream, and even though I want that, too—God, how much do I want that, let me count the ways—Brendan's arrival on the scene came in the nick of time.

"We can't do this." I grope for clothes in my newly organized drawers, while keeping one eye on Tanner, needing to get him on board the self-control train. "Seriously. If we do this, you're going to be in the shit house with your team, and I'm going to be in the shit house with myself. And then we'll both be in the shit house, and all for nothing because this is never going to work."

"It felt like it was working just fine," he says, standing to watch the show as I struggle into a tank top and try not to trip myself stepping into my panties. "It felt like something you needed. Or did I imagine the part where you were begging me to fuck you?"

I shake my head as my entire face flushes hot. "That wouldn't have happened if I hadn't ended up unexpectedly naked in your presence, and that won't happen again." I find shorts and pull them on as fast as I can. "Let's consider this a close brush with disaster, forget it ever happened, and move on as friends."

His eyebrows do a slow-motion crawl up his forehead. "Forget that I was about two seconds away from being inside you?"

"It sounds hard now, but—"

"It is hard now. Hard and ready to get you off as soon as you tell your brother to go home and get your ass back in that bed."

Damn, he's good with the dirty talk, too. Good and dirty and ready to deliver. The strained front of his shorts leaves no doubt about that.

And woah, but do I want what he's offering. I want to jump back into bed with him and fuck him until I forget my own name. Until I forget my ugly history and my bad taste in men and my worse judgment in knowing when to hold 'em and when to fold 'em.

But instead I back toward the door, aiming a firm finger at Tanner's beautiful bare chest. "We can't. This was a mistake."

"It didn't—"

"Blame your pig because it's all her fault," I cut in. I can't let him talk anymore. I'm weak and vulnerable to persuasion, which means I need to get out of this house. "I'm going to get ice cream with Brendan. Do you want me to bring you something? A pint of friendly-flavored peace offering, perhaps?"

"No." His gaze bores into mine with enough heat to make my fresh panties damp between the legs. "Thank you."

"O-okay," I stammer, confused. His lips are saying the appropriate things, but the look in his eyes is saying "I'm going to pin you against the wall and fuck you until your bones turn to jelly."

I guess we'll have to call that good enough.

"See you later, then." The words emerge in a breathless rush as I turn, fleeing down the stairs.

I'm seconds from the bottom, about to make my break for freedom, when Wanda appears out of nowhere, positioning her chubby body at the base of the stairs. She's on another mission of evil, but I'm prepared for her this time.

Jaw clenched, I leap into the air, doing a split leap off the third step and sailing over the pig to land safely on the other side.

"Ha! Take that, pig!" I shout as I dash across the room, pursued by the pitter-patter of little hooves. But I'm too fast for her. Before Wanda can catch up with any bitable part of me, I'm out the door, scampering down the porch steps to where Brendan waits on the walk, tapping something into his phone.

"Let's hit it," I pant, grabbing his arm and towing him toward the SUV.

"Where are we going?" he asks, abandoning his text message.

"Ice cream. I could really use an ice cream right now, how about you?"

Or something else cold enough to cool me the hell off, I add silently.

"I could go for ice cream." Brendan pauses by the passenger's side door, glancing down. "But don't you want to get some shoes on first?"

"Nah, barefoot is good." I haul the door open, hop into the car, and reach for my seatbelt. "We can go to the drive-in near your place. I won't even have to get out."

"All right." He holds up his phone as he walks around to the driver's side. "You mind if I text Laura and Chloe, see if they want to join us?"

I shake my head, casting a sneaky glance toward the door, an irrational part of me certain I won't be safe from my own weakness until Brendan and I are away from this house and all the forbidden things that nearly happened here. That *would have* happened if my brother were the kind of person who worried about dropping by unannounced.

"Yeah, invite them," I say as Brendan slides into the SUV. "I'll bitch about my interview on the way over. I can't promise to keep my language child-friendly if I wait until we've ordered to talk."

"I don't blame you." Brendan's expression grows stormy. "Those women sounded like real pieces of work."

"Bitches is a good word," I say. "Or the c-word."

"Snot goblin is Chloe's favorite new insult," Brendan says as he texts Laura, using ice cream emojis because love has made him thirty-percent cheesier than he was before. "Apparently you can get away with saying snot in the first grade, but not boogers."

I tsk disapprovingly. "Really? What is the world coming to, that a child can't call a booger by its rightful name? What the heck is she supposed to call it?"

"I don't know." He starts the engine and glances over his shoulder. "You'll have to ask her."

"I will." I begin to breathe easier as Brendan clears the driveway and pulls away from the house. "She always has good answers to questions like that."

"She does." Brendan smiles and reaches out to pat my knee. "And don't worry about the snot goblin bitches. You're going to find a job you love and people you love working for. You're too talented to be unemployed for more than a month or two. And you're too good a person to waste your time with shallow losers with fucked up priorities."

"Thanks, big brother," I say softly, feeling lucky to have

him, and lucky that this is my second pep talk in less than an hour.

In addition to making me forget my misery with kisses and his epic chest, Tanner said all the right things. Even more importantly, he seemed to mean every kind, generous word.

I wince as I remember the other business I left unfinished at my new abode. "Fuck!"

"What?" Brendan asks, dividing his attention between me and the road.

"Can I use your phone? I left mine at home, and I need to warn Tanner about something."

Brendan scowls, but nods. "Sure. You mind telling me what?"

"Just roomie stuff," I say vaguely as I snatch Brendan's phone from the cup holder between us and text: *Don't go in your bedroom! I'll come get rid of the creepy Things that Shall Not Be Named as soon as I get home. I won't be more than an hour or so. Sorry again. I promise not to step over the line with pranks or anything else from here on out. This is Diana, by the way. I borrowed Brendan's phone.*

I hit send and then immediately delete the message from Brendan and Tanner's chat history, which seems mostly to include dates and times for scrimmages and meeting up for beers. Though there is something further up—Tanner offering sincere, heartfelt congratulations on Brendan's engagement—that hints at a deeper than casual relationship.

And at Tanner being more of a romantic than I suspected...

"Are you looking through my texts?" Brendan asks.

"Why?" I scroll faster, looking for more evidence of this Not Afraid to Be Sweet Even with his Guy Friends Tanner. "Are you and Nowicki having some kind of secret bromance you're afraid I might find out about?"

"No. I just don't like having nosy sister types poking around in my private messages. Shut it down."

Before I can protest that I'm not poking in his business—I'm just curious about my new roommate and want to nose around in his business—Tanner texts back—*Gotcha. No worries. I'm going to head to the gym, anyway.*

Frowning, I text back—*Didn't you just get back from scrimmage and a bike ride?*

After a moment, he replies—*I suddenly find myself with the need to let off some steam. Though if you would rather I stay here until you get back, I'm happy to wait right where I am. Right where you left me...*

No, that's fine, I tap out quickly, pulse spiking as the drive-in comes into view. *Go let off steam, and we'll get back on the right track tomorrow. Oh, and I'm deleting these texts right now. You should do the same. Talk later.*

I hit send and then delete the chat history, tossing the phone back into the cup holder as Brendan pulls into the stall at the end of the drive-in's second row of spaces. Before he can cut the engine, another text pops through, but thankfully it's just Laura and Chloe, saying they're biking over to meet us in a few minutes.

Brendan and I order sparkling raspberry-flavored water —another drive-in specialty—and talk job interview hell for a few minutes, waiting to order our ice cream until the rest of our group arrives. But I'm no longer angry or hurt enough to rant for more than a few minutes, and the conversation soon turns to wedding plans and honeymoon plans and all the other happy things my brother has on his mind.

And for the first time in a long while, the fact that he's wearing love-colored glasses doesn't bother me. I don't have one bitter or cynical thought. That, as much as anything else that's happened this afternoon, assures me that I made the right decision running from Tanner.

Letting go of cynicism is fine, but starting to think love-colored glasses are acceptable accessories is another. My brother can afford to be besotted—he's got excellent taste in women, and Laura is a total keeper—but I am a different creature, one that should keep her eyes open, uncovered, and on the lookout for danger.

Especially the kind of danger that comes calling in beautiful, green-eyed, chisel-chested packages.

CHAPTER NINE

From the texts of Tanner Nowicki
and Alexei Petrov

PETROV: Hey, my housecleaner is here. Should I have her put fresh sheets on the bed in the pool house before she leaves?

NOWICKI: No thanks, man. I appreciate the offer, but I have to stay here and take care of Wanda. She's got some aggression issues I need to get under control before they get any worse.

PETROV: I have a good method for dealing with pig aggression…

NOWICKI: Don't even start. This pig is a friend, not food.

PETROV: Do your best to remember the other female in your house is just a friend, too. Though I confess I don't have much hope for you.

NOWICKI: Oh yeah, why's that?

PETROV: The titanium plate on my collarbone is aching.
It knows when there's trouble on the horizon.

NOWICKI: That's kind of superstitious, don't you think?

PETROV: I'm Russian. We understand the importance of omens. Your destiny is only partially under your control, rookie. That's why it's important to make wise choices and to remove temptation from your path whenever possible.
Are you sure you don't want to come crash at the pool house?
I'll let you bring your pig if you need something to snuggle with at night.

NOWICKI: That's very generous.

PETROV: Yeah, well, you play a solid two-way game.
I'd like you to stick around for a while, and that's more likely to happen if the team captain isn't out for your blood.

Nowicki: Understood. I've got this under control. No worries.

Petrov: Right, and like my grandmother says—your elbow seems close to your mouth, but you can't bite it.

Nowicki: What?

Petrov: Some things seem easy when they are, in fact, impossible.

Nowicki: Thanks for the pep talk.

Petrov: Any time. And I'll have Georgina change those sheets, just in case.

CHAPTER TEN

DIANA

Come the weekend, I'm starting to feel semi-normal again, figuring it's okay to stop rushing straight to my room as soon as I get home (or as soon as I hear Tanner's car in the drive) to avoid ripping my roomie's clothes off with my teeth, when Tanner texts from the backyard.

Hey. Can you take a break and come down to the pool for a few minutes? I wanted to try one of those pig discipline techniques I've been reading about.

Frowning first at my phone, then at the closed curtains blocking my view of the pool and the man out there in a chest-revealing swimsuit, I text back, *I'm in the middle of color correcting a bunch of wedding photos I need to get back to my friend by tomorrow morning. Rain check until later?*

"Preferably at a time when you're wearing a shirt," I mutter, tossing the phone back onto my desk and squinting at the tiny photos of Pepto-Bismol-pink bridesmaids I'm batch editing in an attempt to correct the bride's poor taste in wedding party attire. The color is truly horrendous, and the puffed sleeves on the dresses only add insult to injury.

God, these poor women...

I'm considering adding a filter to the entire shoot and hoping I can find one that will compliment the skin tones of the many ethnicities represented in the bridal party, when my phone dings again—

I'm not sure conditions will be optimal later. Just pop down for a second? It shouldn't take long, and I'll make you a latte after, as a reward for helping with pig training.

A latte. Damn, that sounds good.

The ghosting-while-Tanner-is-home policy has led to a marked drop in caffeine consumption, since the coffee machine lives in the kitchen and I've been hiding out upstairs. Surely I'll be able to resist the siren's call of my roommate's lickable chest if I focus on the equally tempting lure of caffeine waiting for me as soon as I've completed my pig wrangling duties.

A latte is every bit as delicious as an eight-pack belonging to an excessively fit man who has made it clear he wants nothing more in life than to fuck me until I come my brains out.

Right?

"You're an idiot. Don't go down there," I mutter, even as I put my computer screen to sleep and text Tanner a quick: *be right down.*

I have to prove that I can resist temptation sooner or later, and there's always the chance that Wanda will bite me again and I'll be bleeding too much to care about Tanner's chest. Or his thick, bitable biceps. Or all his other parts that I'm not going to think about because thinking about them is a bad, bad idea.

After a quick glance around the living room to be sure Wanda isn't lying in wait, I breeze into the kitchen and out into the backyard, where the late afternoon air is filled with the smell of roses, chlorine, and grilled hot dogs from a barbeque somewhere farther down the block.

Distant laughter, softly competing soundtracks from various Sunday afternoon parties, and the squeals of kids running through the sprinkler across the street add to the idyllic summer day vibe. As I pad barefoot down the stone path to the pool, I find myself thinking about long days at the beach as a kid, when my sisters and I would spend hours climbing the tree that stretched out over the water near Hidden Beach and hurling ourselves into the frigid ocean below. Sometimes it was so cold that for a split second, right as your head plunged beneath the waves, the shock of the chill would trigger an out-of-body experience.

For a moment, I would forget who I was, where I was, what I was, hovering frozen in a place beyond body or identity, where there is only friendly darkness and the soft surprise of encountering that primal, eternal spark that remains when everything else is gone. I tried to explain that spark to Brendan once, but at ten I didn't have the words to describe it in a way that made sense. I only knew that I lived for that scary, beautiful moment when a force of nature beyond my control made me forget everything but my essential me-ness.

I round the corner to spy the stunning man standing in the shade at the far end of the pool, and my heart does a leap-flicker in my chest that I will myself to ignore. This force of nature is firmly within my control, and there's no way I'm jumping into the deep end with Tanner.

I'm staying on dry land, where a woman who is incapable of navigating the stormy waters of relationships belongs.

Tanner spots me as I step off the path and motions me over, pressing a finger to his lips. When I'm close enough, he points to the pig asleep in the grass behind his now-empty lounge chair and whispers, "She's asleep so this is the perfect time."

"The perfect time for what?" I whisper back.

"To play move the pig," he says, smiling.

"Move the pig…" I cast a wary look Wanda's way. "That sounds like a game that ends in lost fingers. Or an arm. Maybe a spleen."

"Not if we start when she's calm and relaxed." Tanner places a warm hand at the small of my back, urging me closer to the sleeping menace. "Moving other pigs around is what dominant pigs do to show that they're in charge of the herd. So when Wanda wakes up to find you moving her from one spot to another, she'll instinctively realize that you're dominant and that it's not okay to bite you or rush you or ambush you in the bathroom."

My eyebrows creep higher. "Or, instead, she realizes that I touched her while she was sleeping and decides to gnaw my face off."

"No, she won't." Tanner pats my hip in what I assume is supposed to be an encouraging fashion, but it only makes me feel inappropriately tingly. "You're going to move her with your legs. She won't be anywhere near your face."

"Oh, well, that's comforting," I huff, but I can't help returning his grin.

Ugh, he's so pretty when he's smiling and half-naked, with his golden skin glistening with a mixture of sweat and sunscreen and his black swim trunks sitting so low on his hips I can almost see a hint of—

Look away from the happy trail, Diana! Look away!

With a concentrated act of will, I force my gaze back to Tanner's eyes. "You really think this will work?"

"Probably not the first time, but everything I've read says that continuing to move her regularly—always when she's relaxed—will shift her perception of you and eventually transform the relationship. She'll realize that you're in charge and that she's not top dog anymore."

"Or top hog," I quip.

He smiles again, rewarding me way too easily and sending my heart into flutter-flicker mode all over again. "Exactly. You'll be top hog, which will make Wanda feel safe and secure and lead to reduced aggression."

I shake my head. "Why is that?"

"Pigs like to know whose boss, I guess," he says with a shrug. "No matter how tough they play it, they secretly enjoy giving up control to someone bigger, stronger, and better able to protect the herd."

My eyes narrow and Tanner smiles, a grin wicked enough to assure me I wasn't imagining the teasing lilt in his voice.

"Don't get any ideas." I point a warning finger at his chest.

His grin widens. "Like what?"

"I don't need anyone bigger and stronger to protect me or my herd."

"I never said you did," he insists before adding in a silkier voice, "But giving up control can be nice, don't you think? Every once in a while?"

I swallow hard and debate running back to the house. On the one hand, that would leave no doubt in Tanner's mind that I'm still tempted by all the yumminess he has to offer. On the other hand, it would remove me from the source of temptation before I confess how many times I've daydreamed about riding him like a rodeo cowboy the past three days.

I'm turning to make a break for it when Tanner steps in, laying a hand on my shoulder. "Don't be scared. I'll be right beside you. You can do this. I won't let her hurt you again. I promise."

It's not her I'm worried about, I think. Aloud I say, "Okay. Fine. What do I do?"

It would be nice to not be afraid of at least one of my roommates. If I can make peace with Wanda, then there will only be one threat lurking in the house, tempting me to forget what's best for me and drown my new-to-the-city blues with sex, sex, and more sex that I have no doubt won't remain casual. Tanner isn't a casual guy. He's a get-under-your-skin, invade-your-dreams, tempt-your-heart-into-the-emotion-ocean kind of guy.

"You're going to nudge your feet under her rump and then shuffle forward," he says, guiding me closer to Wanda's slumbering form, "moving her along the grass with your shins."

"You're sure this isn't going to piss her off?" I ask, palms beginning to sweat even though Wanda is adorable when she's sleeping. Looking at her now, with her gently closed eyes and softly smiling mouth, you would never guess she's a domestic terrorist with a rabid hunger for the blood of her rivals.

"Not according to what I've read," Tanner says. "You just want to keep applying firm, insistent pressure in a friendly way."

I shake my hands at my sides, trying to loosen up. "And exactly how do I make friendly with my shins?"

"Not with your shins, with your voice. Talk to her, tell her she's a good little pig but it's time to move along because you're the boss."

"Right. Okay." I fight a burst of hysterical laughter as I wiggle my bare toes under Wanda's bottom, wishing I were wearing shoes. She's a clean pig, but having something covering my toes in case she wakes up and decides to lunge at my exposed flesh would be nice.

"Once you start, keep moving until she backs away from you," Tanner whispers from too close behind me, making me feel pinned between a pig and a hard place. A rock-hard place that smells of coconut sunscreen, chlorine, and warm, sexy man.

Why does he have to be so fucking delicious in every way?

Why, why, why?

"If she turns and goes to sit down somewhere else, that's even better," he continues in a deep, husky voice. "That means she's fully accepted your dominance."

"I've always wanted someone to fully accept my dominance," I murmur.

"Really?" He sounds intrigued.

I glance over my shoulder, my breath catching when I see how close his lips are to mine. "No, not really, Tanner. But I do have a question."

"Yes?" His gaze drifts from my eyes to my mouth, making me tingle in places I shouldn't.

My tongue slips out to dampen my lips, and my pulse leaps. "If Wanda decides I'm dominant, where does that leave you?"

"I'll be another submissive member of the herd," he says. "But I'm okay with that. She loves me too much to bite me, even if I'm submissive to the lady of the house."

I shake my head, torn between laughter and the urge to press up onto my toes and kiss him for being an adorable weirdo. "This may be the strangest conversation I've ever had."

"Doubtful. I was there for the killer mermaids, remember."

My breath rushes out in a soft laugh. "True. You were. I'm glad they didn't get you."

"Me, too. Now quit stalling and start shuffling, Daniels."

"Yes, sir." I catch a flash of heat in his eyes before I shift my focus back to Wanda, enough to make me wonder if Tanner would like someone to accept his dominance. And for the first time in my life, the idea isn't a complete turn off.

I could see myself calling him "sir," as long as he promised to pin me to my mattress and bang my brains out after.

Dangerous thoughts, girl. So many dangerous thoughts...

Struggling valiantly to focus on the task at hand instead of the tempting mountain of a man behind me, I move forward, nudging Wanda along the grass with my shins. After only a moment, she snuffles in her sleep and gives a full body shudder, making me freeze and my hands curl into panicked fists at my sides.

"Keep going," Tanner whispers. "Slow, steady, and friendly. Don't forget to be friendly."

"Friendly. Right," I mutter through clenched teeth before adding in an upbeat voice, "Good pig, Wanda! You're a good little pig."

"And keep moving," Tanner urges. "Moving and friendly at the same time."

"I'm going to kill you," I growl, pulse skipping a beat as Wanda grunts in irritation. "You and your pig. Both of you. And then I'm going to make bacon, invite everyone over for a BBQ, and take a poll on which of you tastes better."

Tanner's hands settle on my hips. "It'll be Wanda. My percentage of body fat is too low for me to make decent bacon."

"Is that a humble brag?"

"Just follow my lead." His arm slips around my waist. "I've got you."

Before I can protest, Tanner shuffles forward behind me, and I'm propelled into motion once more, a now wakeful Wanda grunt-grumbling in surprise as she's pushed onto her feet.

"Good little pig." Tanner moves us along faster, sending my shins bumping into Wanda's backside. "Good pig, but it's time to move along. Move on pig. Move on."

"Move on, pig," I echo, gaining confidence as Wanda

plods across the grass without turning to tear a hole in my knee. "Move on, little pig."

"Such a good pig." Tanner's hands are on my hips again, guiding me away from the warmth of his body.

"So good, but don't look back, because I'm the boss," I say sweetly. "I'm the big bad pig boss and it's time for you to move on and find another place to be, Miss Thing."

Tanner laughs as he releases me, sending me wobbling along like a kid riding a bike without training wheels for the first time.

For a moment, my heart jumps into my throat and my fear returns, but I push through the rush of anxiety, remaining focused on my shuffling and cooing until Wanda finally picks up speed, scampering away to root in the raised planter bed where Tanner buries carrots for her every morning. She simply trots quietly away, without biting or lunging or showing the slightest sign of shifty-eyed, sneaky, pig evil.

Chest swelling with pride, I turn back to Tanner with a grin and whisper excitedly, "I did it! I moved the pig!"

"You did," he says, his smile as big as mine.

"She accepted my dominance!" I crow softly, thrusting my arms overhead in a V for victory.

"She totally did. You are the dominant pig in this herd, woman. How does it feel?"

I press my lips together, fighting a giggle and losing. "Good." I bring my hands up to cover my goofy grin as I add, "Really good, actually. Is that weird?"

"Not weird at all." Tanner steps in until he's standing so close I have to tip my head back to hold his gaze. "It's sexy."

"You get off on watching me relocate your pig?"

"No, it's your smile." The mixture of heat and vulnerability in his eyes makes it impossible to look away. "It's one of the best smiles I've ever seen. Bright and beautiful and fearless."

"I'm not fearless," I confess, swaying closer. "Not even close."

"But you could—" His words end in a soft *humph* of surprise as a warm, solid body shoves between our legs.

We look down and Wanda looks up, grunting as she backs away only to rush forward again, ramming between our legs a second time.

I arch a brow. "I think Wanda wants us to make room for the Holy Spirit."

"Wanda can go away." Tanner reaches down, shoving Wanda's shoulder gently, but firmly. "Go away, Wanda." She advances and he pushes her again, sending her stumbling back on startled hooves. "Go away! Bad pig."

Wanda stands trembling at the edge of the pool, clearly shocked, and emits a plaintive oink.

"Go away." Tanner points to the rooting garden, muttering to me, "Shoulder shoving is for when they show aggression. You're not supposed to talk nice after the shoulder shoving."

Wanda takes a tentative step forward, but Tanner stops her with another no-nonsense command. "Go away! Right now. Bad pig."

After a long searching look that clearly communicates "How could you do this to me? How could you let that worthless blond human come between us and our perfect love?" Wanda hangs her head and waddles away to a patch of shade on the far side of the pool.

"Poor thing," I whisper, fighting a laugh as she dramatically flops into a patch of dust beneath the tree. "I would feel sorry for her if she weren't such a butt-biting bully."

Tanner turns back to me. "Don't feel sorry for her. This is her karma. She deserves every bit of what's coming to her."

My smile vanishes, dropping away like a wild child

leaping from the safety of the trees into the churning surf below.

"Did I say something wrong?" Tanner asks, reading me with an accuracy that's unnerving, considering we've only known each other a week.

I shake my head. "I just don't like the idea of karma. It makes those of us with lousy luck think we must have done something to deserve it. And I really don't think I did." I shrug uncomfortably, trying to force lightness into my tone and failing. "But maybe I was Genghis Kahn in my last life."

"You weren't Genghis Kahn." Tanner lifts a hand, capturing a rogue curl that escaped from my messy bun and looping it around his finger. "I didn't mean karma in that way. I'm not one of those 'everything happens for a reason' people."

"Good. I hate those people."

His lips curve. "Tell me how you really feel."

"I did," I say, wishing I had the strength to untangle his hand from my hair and step away. "But you won't listen."

"Actions speak louder than words, Daniels," he says, a challenge in his voice. "You say we can't get close, but you're still standing here feeling up my chest."

My eyes widen, but before I can protest that I'm doing no such thing, I realize that my hands have indeed found their way to Tanner's chest, where my fingers are sensuously tracing the rise and fall of his muscles and growing increasingly slippery with sunscreen.

I curse, Tanner grins, and before I have time to remind myself—or him—what a bad idea this is, I'm in his arms, kissing him like the world's about to end. My fingers dig into his shoulders, my legs wrap tight around his hips as he lifts me into the air, and I put up exactly zero fight as he crosses the lawn, opens the door to the detached garage, and steps into the dim cool of a shadowy place where we are free to get as naked as we please.

And so we do.

Before I quite know what's happened, Tanner is lifting me up to sit on something smooth with a hint of an incline. I turn to see what I'm perched on, but Tanner chooses that moment to rip open the Velcro close on his swim trunks. And then he's as naked as I am, and I have eyes for nothing but the golden god moving between my legs, his erection so thick and delicious I can't resist the urge to reach down and stroke him, up and down, relishing the thick, burning, clearly-wild-for-me length pulsing beneath my fingers.

"Your cock is a beautiful little bastard." My words become a gasp as he cups my breasts in his sun-warmed hands and pinches my nipples, sending electric shocks of need coursing between my legs.

"Rethink your adjectives, Daniels."

"I think cocks can be beautiful, don't you?" I ask innocently, deliberately misunderstanding him.

He hums as he kisses his way down my throat, the rumble vibrating across my skin. "That wasn't the adjective I was talking about, but that's all right. I have ways of proving you wrong, little girl."

I shiver, threading my fingers into his hair as he sucks my nipple into his mouth and sticky waves of desire throb through my bloodstream. "Is that supposed to scare me?"

"Never," he says, making my belly flutter as his fingers replace his mouth, continuing to pluck and caress my charged skin. "I don't want to scare you, Beach Pixie. I just want to make you come. That's all I've wanted since the night I first kissed you."

I reach for him again, already as desperate for him as I was the last time we were naked together. "Birth control is covered, and I'm clean. You?"

He groans as I wrap my fingers around his cock, squeezing tight. "Clean, but I don't want to rush. I want this to last."

"Make it last next time," I say, breath coming faster as I scoot forward.

"But I—"

"It's been a long time for me," I confess, fitting the swollen head of him to where I'm so wet and ready. "A really long time. Please don't make me wait. I need this. I need *you*."

The last word turns out to be the magic one.

A moment later, Tanner pushes inside me, filling me with his thick, hot, not-little-at-all cock, and we proceed to take each other with an intensity that is anything but restrained. We gasp and cling and strain closer, deeper, faster, harder, until I'm floating, falling, exploding like the firework that fell behind the shelf and was lost in the dark for so long it feared it would never join the rest of its brothers and sisters in the sky.

But now I'm there, bursting open in the dark, dizzy and sparkling and biting Tanner's full bottom lip as I soar. Catching fire.

And God, it's so good. It's so right and sweet and hot that for a long time I can't think about anything but Tanner and his taste, his touch, and all the crazy wonderful things he's making me feel.

By the time I realize the dings and pings filling the air are coming from the pinball machine I'm sitting on—not from orgasm-induced auditory hallucinations—I've come twice and am greedily reaching, climbing, praying for number three.

"I think we're going to get a high score," I gasp against Tanner's lips.

"Hell yes, we are," he says, groaning as he adds, "Fuck, I'm going to come, baby. I'm going to come so fucking hard."

"Inside me, inside me," I demand, digging my nails into the thick muscles of his ass as he pumps deeper, faster, building the swelling tension until I spiral out a third time just as his cock begins to jerk and twitch.

We kiss and moan and make happy, humming celebration sounds for several minutes after the main event, until we both suddenly start laughing for reasons that defy explanation.

But it doesn't matter why we're giggly. All that matters is that this was good. So good. So good that we already know we're going to do it again.

And again.

And again…

First on a blanket we spread on the floor of the garage, then on the pinball machine again before we sneak out to jump naked into the pool as the sun is setting. We christen the shallow end—being sure to stay hidden from the neighbor's view beneath the benevolent trees—before heading back into the garage to pillage beer from the beer fridge and play pinball naked.

Tanner wins two out of three games and rewards himself by decreeing that he gets to go down on me first, which he does, with great skill and enthusiasm while I writhe beneath him, watching the stars come out through the skylight while Tanner reminds me what I've been missing.

"So much," I murmur after I've returned the favor and we're lying sticky, sweaty, and happy as pigs in a pile of pink blankets on the floor of the garage. "I've missed sex so, so much."

"Me, too," he says with a blissed out sigh. "It had been a while for me, too. Especially since…"

I prop up on one arm, gazing down into his shadowed face. "Since what?"

His fingers skim up and down the valley of my spine,

making me shiver. "Since it was this good. You're amazing when you're naked."

I try to stop my grin by biting my lip and fail. "Thank you. You're not bad yourself."

He scowls. "Not bad?"

"Good, I meant," I say, smile widening. "I mean, I think so. I find my memory is fuzzy for some reason. Maybe you could refresh it for me?"

So he does, and it's so much better than good.

So much better that by the time we finally head to bed, I'm too exhausted to worry too much about the danger of making your roommate and your fuck buddy the same person, or to stress about the warm feeling that fills my chest as Tanner curls around me in my bed, pressing a kiss to the top of my head before we fall deeply, profoundly asleep.

CHAPTER ELEVEN

DIANA

One week later...

VOICE MESSAGE: Pick up the phone, Amanda. I have something very important to discuss with you. This can't be done via text, okay? Seriously, this is voice-activated information only.

I'll call back in five minutes. Pick up.

Two minutes later...

VOICEMAIL MESSAGE: I couldn't wait five minutes. I need to talk to you now. Why aren't you answering the phone? Why can't you compromise with me, woman? I promise I won't call you again for an entire month if you'll pick up the phone the next time I call okay?

Pretty please with sugar on top?

Because you love me and understand sometimes I need to hear a voice aside from the one in my head?

Okay, I'm calling back in five minutes. Talk to you then.

Three minutes later...

Voicemail message: Oh my God, please pick up the phone! I know you're not at work because I called the hospital and they said you were off today. Please, Amanda, I'm freaking out, and I need to talk to someone. I can't talk to my brother because he'll lose his shit if he finds out I'm sleeping with someone on his team, and I can't talk to Carly because she's happy and in love and doesn't understand my need to not sleep with guys I think I could have feelings for.

But I can't do this again. I seriously can't.

Only I don't know if I can stop…

This guy has a magical dick, Mandy. His dick is like a unicorn. His dick has basically proven the existence of unicorns. I now believe in unicorns. For real, I'm not kidding.

Call me back, please.

Please, please, please!

* * *

I end the call with a sigh, flop back into the hammock in the shade at the edge of the backyard, and take another drag on my rapidly dwindling joint, my clenched jaw relaxing as the migraine that's been clawing away at my skull all morning finally recedes.

But it will be back. I have no doubt about that.

I'm finished with the wedding photo processing and color

correction work from my friend Jill, who is a wedding photographer in Seattle, and she paid me promptly, but that's only going to keep me in groceries for a week or two. I have to find a full-time job. I've sent out what feels like a gazillion resumes, but so far I've only received one glimmer of interest aside from the disastrous fashion interview, and that job—PR for a pair of ski resorts—isn't interviewing until October.

By October I will be broke.

"Flat-ass broke," I confess to the oak leaves waving gently overhead, wondering if the phrase comes from being so poor that you can't afford food so your ass gradually deflates until you're just skin, bones, and saggy cheeks where your formerly bodacious backside used to be.

And of course, thinking of bodacious asses makes me think of Tanner and how insanely hot it was to watch his ass muscles clench in the bathroom mirror while he fucked me in the shower last night. Before I can warn my brain to take it easy, I'm so turned on by the erotic walk down memory lane that I know exactly how I'll be greeting my roomie when he gets home.

I promised myself that today would be the day I tell Tanner we have to tap the brakes on the non-stop fuck-fest, but I am clearly helpless to resist the man.

"Magical unicorn penis," I whisper to the leaves, which flutter faster in response because they get it. They totally get it.

Amanda will probably get it, too. In the early days, she dubbed her boyfriend Arnold "Wonderdick" because his dick was wonderful and so was he. But as time passed and Arnold turned out to be an emotionally manipulative, commitment-phobic ass-hat, his name came to mean something else.

At least to me. Now Wonderdick refers to the fact that he's basically a superhero jerk.

But Mandy keeps getting back together with the

schmuck. She literally seems helpless to resist him, no matter how bad things ended between them the last time they broke up.

Is that what's going to happen to me if I stay here and keep falling onto Tanner's magical penis every chance I get? Will I eventually get hooked on him like a drug? Or worse, will I betray the promises I made to myself and let feelings into the picture?

Just the thought of it is enough to send a cold wave of panic washing through my happy buzz. I can't do feelings. I just can't. Feelings always end the same way—in disaster—and as an unemployed nearly-thirty-year-old in the midst of a quarter-life crisis, I can't do disaster right now.

I grab my phone, intending to call Amanda again and leave such a long, desperate message that she'll have to call me back—or at least feel like a sorry excuse for a human being for refusing to pick up—when Tanner's face suddenly appears overhead, prompting the leaves behind him to dance happily in the breeze.

"Shit," I breathe, laughing as I let my phone fall back onto the hammock beside me. "You scared me."

"How's the headache?" He sits down, making the hammock sink and my hips slide his way.

"Better." I hold out the remains of my joint. "Want to put that out for me?"

Tanner takes the gently smoking nub and stabs it out in the grass before turning back to me and laying a hand on my thigh. It's a proprietary hand, one that asserts ownership, or at least stewardship, over my body.

But before I can sort out why that's not as troubling as it should be, Tanner says, "I've got a surprise for you," and happy bubbles fizz through my bloodstream, distracting me.

Because what, I ask you, is more wonderful than a surprise? Especially when you're a little buzzed? Not only is the surprise itself a fun thing, but there's also the fact that someone went to the trouble to arrange to surprise you, which is also lovely and thoughtful.

"What kind of surprise?" I thread my fingers together in a fist I press to my chest. "Is it a kitten?"

He grins. "No, it's not a kitten. Wanda's still adjusting to not being ruler of the roost. I don't think she's ready for a kitten."

I wrinkle my nose. "Good point. And as one of the underemployed, I can't commit to being a cat mom right now. Because kittens become cats, Tanner. Cats who want to eat all the food and get taken to the vet. That's a fact."

"They do," he agrees. "But there might be cat mom level employment in your future before you know it. I got a lead on a job you would be perfect for today. I thought we could go check out one of the company locations tonight, and see if you think it might be a good fit."

I sit up, blinking fast. As if that will do anything to banish my buzz. "Shit. I can't meet anyone right now. My hair is a disaster, and I can't be trusted not to say crazy things when I'm high."

He frowns. "So you're saying that killer mermaids aren't real?"

"Of course they are," I say seriously. "You would be dead right now if I hadn't stayed on the beach and made out with your face to protect you. You basically owe me your life."

"That's why I'm trying to return the favor." He scoots behind me, rearranging the pillows and then pulling me back against him. "And you won't have to meet anyone tonight. Just come hang out, have dinner and a beer with me, and see if you like the vibe. If so, I can call my friend Jax and get you an interview next week. He's looking to hire a PR person with a strong background in photography and graphic design."

I relax against his chest, turning to look up into his stupidly handsome face. Why does he have to be so pretty to look at? It would be so much easier to not fall on his penis if he had nose warts, or at least some mild eczema or something.

"What do you think?" he continues, brushing my humidity-frizzed hair from my face. "You up for some dinner and beer?"

"That sounds like a date," I say, eyes narrowing.

He strokes my hair again, petting me while making a soft shushing sound. "It's okay. Relax your squirrely brain. We can eat together in a public place without putting labels on things, I promise."

I scrunch my nose and purse my lips, determined not to smile or otherwise encourage this easy, flirty thing he's trying to pull. "This is sex, Tanner. Magical unicorn-penis sex, and that's it."

His dimples pop, and I laugh. I can't help it.

"You look so proud of yourself." I press a finger to his cheek.

"Well, it's not every day a guy learns he's got a magical unicorn penis." His hands skim from my waist to cup my breasts through my T-shirt. "Does that mean I'm the chosen one? Do I have to go on a quest or something?"

I arch into his touch as his fingers tease my nipples, awakening the hunger that's always simmering beneath the surface when we're together—hot and ready to boil over at a moment's notice. "Yes, a quest to my bedroom. Where I will remind you why we shouldn't mess with a good thing."

"Maybe I don't want to wait that long," he whispers as he begins to gather my skirt in one hand, drawing it slowly up my legs.

"We can't have sex in this part of the backyard," I hiss, even as I reach back for the close of his shorts. "What about

Mr. Pickering the Pervert? We're in clear view of his window."

"I have a confession to make." The hem of my skirt reaches my upper thighs, and I shiver, anticipating the moment Tanner realizes I'm not wearing underwear.

"What's that?" I stroke his cock through his boxer briefs, loving how easy it is to get him hard.

"There is no Mr. Pickering. The people who live next door are the Yergers, and they go to Maine every summer. No one's going to see a thing that happens in this backyard."

My jaw drops. "You dirty liar!"

I turn to give him a piece of my mind for creating an imaginary pervert, but before I can tell him he's the worst, he's kissing me, his tongue stroking against mine, reminding me he's actually the best.

Oh God, he's the very, *very* best, which he proves by taking me from behind in the hammock—slow and hot and dizzy, sexy sweet, his fingers gliding over my clit until I come so hard I see stars, even though the sun won't set for hours.

"You're a goddamned American hero," I sigh as we're catching our breath after, with my skirt still bunched up at my waist and his cock going soft inside me.

"Why's that?" He kisses my temple.

"We didn't fall out of the hammock. And that was all you, friend, because I'm pretty sure I was doing nothing to help the balance situation."

He hums, his lips still warm on my skin. "I'm not going to let you fall, Beach Pixie. You're precious cargo to be handled with care."

I don't know if it's the weed making me emotional or the fact that Tanner's still inside me at this very second, making me very *literally* connected to him, but for a second I think I'm going to cry. I haven't cried over boy stuff in so long—not even when Darby, my last steady hipster man-bun boyfriend, bailed while I was on a week-long spelunking photo shoot and I came home to find a Dear Jane note and every credit card I'd been stupid enough to leave in the cabin maxed out to buy camping equipment Darby needed to "find his Zen."

I am accustomed to the men I date turning out to be emotionally unavailable losers or stealing from me or deciding it would be more fun to go home with someone other than the girl they took to the party.

I am not accustomed to this…sweetness.

"It's just sex, Muscle Boy," I whisper, but my throat is so tight he doesn't hear me.

Or maybe he simply pretends not to hear, because a few minutes later, after we've both rearranged our clothes, he turns to me, leans in close, and says in a dead-serious voice, "If you don't want people to like you, then you need to stop being so fucking adorable, okay, Daniels?"

I shake my head, but I can't pull my gaze away from his. "You remember you hated me a week ago, right?"

"I never hated you. I was frustrated by your inability to see how nice I am or understand that my magical unicorn penis sought only to devote its life to giving you pleasure."

I grin in spite of myself. "You're ridiculous."

"I didn't ask to be the chosen one," he says, solemnly.

I snort with laughter as I slide out of the hammock, wiggling my bare feet in the cool grass. "So how fancy is this eating and drinking beer place? Do I need to shower, or can I get away with slapping on some blush and changing into clothes that don't smell like sex? Because I'll be honest, I'm suddenly quite hungry, and my capacity for caring about being pretty is dwindling rapidly. I already care twenty percent less than I cared when I started this sentence."

He loops an arm around my shoulders, keeping me close as we start toward the house. "You're beautiful just like this. I like the fuzzy sex hair, but if you're determined to change, jeans and a T-shirt will be fine. It's a laid back, pricey microbrew and gourmet burger kind of joint."

Before I can walk back my acceptance of this invitation—the balance in my bank account is way too low to be indulging in pricey *anything*—Tanner says, "My treat. I invited you, so I'm buying. I insist. No arguments. So hurry up and get changed. I'll meet you at the car in five minutes."

I hesitate—this is clearly a date, no ifs, ands, or buts about it—but then my stomach growls and I ignore the voice of reason, justifying the choice because a person can't be expected to be reasonable while they're practically starving to death.

And I haven't eaten since breakfast, so…

I put worry to bed for the night and change into the yellow sundress Tanner likes, then I grab a light sweater, pausing in the bathroom long enough to pull my hair into a less messy bun and sweep on blush, mascara, and lip gloss without making eye contact with my reflection.

It's easier to lie to yourself if you don't make eye contact, and I don't want to face the truth tonight. I want an evening with a gorgeous man who thinks I'm beautiful, a night to pretend I still believe there are a few princes left in a world full of jokers, liars, and thieves.

CHAPTER TWELVE

TANNER

We arrive at Good Timber Brewery's downtown location just after six, in plenty of time to beat the rush and stake out the far corner of the bar, where we've got a clear view of the door and the expansive warehouse style restaurant. The combination of cool, moody light and twenty-foot totem poles scattered throughout the space make Good Timber feel like you've stepped into an enchanted forest on a moonlit night.

And thanks to the high ceilings and redwood paneling on three of the four walls—the fourth is all glass, affording a view of the antique brewing equipment in the adjoining space—the bar and restaurant is one of the few in the trendy downtown area where you can hear your date speak without leaning in to shout in each other's ears.

My date...

I've managed to get Diana out of the house, on a date, and so far she hasn't shouted "prank call," stomped my foot, and made a run for the door.

So far, so good. She's been almost affectionate, in fact, taking my arm after I helped her out of the car and allowing me to pull out her bar stool and scoot it back in. But she mentioned that she'd skipped lunch, so it could be that she's simply too weak with hunger to thwart my attempts at chivalry.

If she weren't already so tiny, I might be tempted to deprive her of food more often. But then, being forced to starve your girlfriend in order to keep her in an affectionate frame of mind probably isn't a good sign.

She's not your girlfriend, dude. She hasn't even agreed to date you on the semi-regular. You need to slow your fucking roll.

The inner voice is giving excellent advice, but I'm not in the mood to listen. I'm in the mood to pretend this person who makes me laugh and think and come like a superhero killing bad guys with the force of my orgasms is starting to find me as addictive as I'm finding her.

"Appetizers ASAP, okay?" Diana runs a finger down the list of pub snacks. "Just so I don't pass out halfway through my first beer?"

"Sounds good." We order crab cakes, grilled fish sliders, and two Tangerine Daydream drafts—the summer seasonal ale that's become my motivation for adding an extra mile to my run every morning—and sit back to take in the relaxed, hippie-hipster vibe.

"I wonder if the animals on the totem poles come to life after the bar closes?" Diana muses, peering over the rim of her chilled pint glass as she takes her first sip. As the cold, citrus-flavored hops slide over her tongue, her eyes widen. "Oh wow. That's amazing. It tastes like beach sunshine."

"Beach sunshine has a different flavor than normal sunshine?"

She scoffs. "Obviously. It's saltier and breezier. Everyone knows that."

"Right. What was I thinking?" I ask, smiling because that's what my face does when I'm with her. Because she's funny, yes, but also because she has a way of teasing that makes me feel like I'm in on the joke.

She brings her glass back to her lips, taking another sip before setting it back on the bar. "Yeah, that is crazy delicious. But don't let me have any more until the food comes. I don't want to embarrass myself at an establishment where I hope to interview someday." She sits up straighter, rubbing her hands together. "So are they looking for someone just for the restaurant? Or for the entire Good Timber brand? They distribute right? I swear I've seen that logo in the beer section at the grocery store."

"They do distribute, but I think the PR job is just for the restaurants. They've got two locations and are opening a third before the end of the summer. Jax has someone doing PR and social media now, but the guy is quitting to stay home with his kids. So Jax needs a replacement in the pipeline soon."

Diana's brows lift. "Good for PR guy. I think it's cool that more families are making choices like that. I mean, why shouldn't the dad stay home with the kids if that makes more sense for the family? Gender roles are so arbitrary anyway." She reaches for her beer but checks herself with a guilty grin. "Nope, not drinking that yet. What about you?"

I blink. "Me?"

"Would you ever want to be a stay-at-home dad?"

I grin. "Why? You looking to knock me up, sexy?"

Diana rolls her eyes, but her cheeks are pinker than they were a second ago. "Of course not. I'm not financially stable enough to have a cat, let alone a kid. I'm just curious. You've got a pretty developed caretaking side for a professional jock. Kind of reminds me of my brother actually."

"Thanks." Warmth spreads through my chest at the unexpected compliment. "I admire Brendan a lot. Even when he's giving me the 'you'd better not touch my sister' side-eye."

Diana grimaces. "He can be protective on occasion. But I'm the same way with him. One time, this girl he was crushing on when we were kids threw the stuffed panda he bought her for Valentine's Day into the school fountain, so I pushed her in after it. I was four years younger and about half her size so she never saw me coming."

"Common theme in your life?"

She grins. "Maybe. So are you going to answer the question or not?"

I shrug. "I don't know. I haven't really thought about it. I mean, I'd like to have kids, but my career is just getting started. I'm so focused on that right now it's hard to imagine what life is going to be like when I leave the NHL."

"That's because you're a baby," she says, reaching for her beer.

I stop her, looping my fingers around her wrist, encircling the delicate bone. "No beer before food," I say, my pulse beating faster as she bites her bottom lip. "And you're only three years older than I am, granny."

She shifts on her stool until her thigh brushes mine, sending another charge of awareness surging across my skin. "Three years is like nine when it's the woman who's older. Girls mature faster than boys. So mentally, I'm practically old enough to be your mother."

"Aren't you the one who just said gender roles are arbitrary?"

Her eyes narrow. "This isn't gender, it's biology and science. Girl's brains optimize connections up to ten years earlier than their male counterparts. We get to the grown-up place faster, it's a scientific fact."

"But you're not a girl." My fingers skim up the back of her calf to tease behind her knee. "And I'm not a boy. I think we proved we're both adults before we left the house tonight."

She cocks her head, eyebrows sending out curious signals.

"What? Ask me anything," I say. "I'm an open book."

Her lips curve as she asks in a soft, almost shy voice, "How old were you the first time?"

"Sixteen." I brush my thumb over her knee where a white, puckered scar testifies to her tomboy years riding her skateboard without kneepads. "You?"

"Nineteen. I looked so young for so long I had a hard time getting guys to take me seriously as a sexual being."

"I take you seriously." As the words leave my mouth, I realize how true they are. In just fourteen days, she's gotten under my skin in a way few people ever have. I'm never going to forget her, even if I fail to convince her that we should give this thing between us more than the summer.

"That's because I put the fear into you early with the mannequins in your bed," she says with a wink.

"That must be it," I agree, grateful that my confession didn't spur another episode of "Push Nowicki Away Before He Gets Attached." I'm not a fan of that show, not even a little bit.

Our food arrives, and in between bites of grilled fish and crab cake, I tell the story of how I met Jax—at my sister's going away party, back when he was dating one of Chey's friends. Diana asks thoughtful questions about the beer and the brewery, and by the time we share one of the massive burgers and order another pint, she's looking positively giddy with optimism.

"Thanks so much for bringing me here," she says, giving my arm a quick squeeze. "It may sound silly, but I've got a good feeling about this. I know promoting beer and national parks seem like wildly different things, but I can already see so many places where the skill sets will overlap. And I love the energy here. I'm so much more comfortable around beer and totem poles than designer dresses and hundred-dollar eye cream"

"I thought you might be," I say, happy because she's happy. I really am a simple creature in some ways, which is good, I guess, since I'm fairly complicated in others.

Which reminds me…

"Be right back." I slide off my stool and head for the men's room, where I pull out my phone and check my to-do list for tonight and tomorrow in private, so Diana won't start accusing me of being addicted to my phone again.

It's a compulsion at this point—I check it ten times a day if not more—but it's the best way I've found to keep myself from getting distracted and falling back into the habit of being late for everything all the time. I'm sure most people can look at their list once or twice and remember what's on the agenda, but an ADHD brain, at least mine, doesn't work that way.

Again, I remember why I started this habit in the first place. I've got "Skype with Chey" on the schedule for eleven p.m.—a sixteen hour time difference between Portland and South Korea makes for some strange chat dates—which means Diana and I should head for home before too long. Traffic gets hairy in town on the weekends, and I need to take Wanda out for her pre-bedtime walk before I get set up at the computer.

I add "call Jax and set up interview for Diana" to my list for tomorrow afternoon at three p.m.—I have to assign each task a time, or everything globs together in my head, and I don't know where to start—and slip my phone into my pocket.

I make my way back to the bar, trying not to think about how many things are on my list for tomorrow, including all the financial shit I've been putting off since last year. The thought of fighting the focus demons so I can talk bills and budget for an hour, even with my financial advisor there to walk me through it, makes me want to throw in my ear buds and go pound pavement. But my summer schedule is cake compared to how hairy things get once the season starts, and not every problem can be solved by cardio.

"Everything okay?" Diana asks as I slide back onto the stool beside her.

I tug out my wallet. "Yeah, just remembered I have a date to check in with my sister at eleven." I motion for the bartender, making the universal scribbling sign for the check.

"Is that all?" She leans in, propping her arms on the bar as she studies my face. "You look stressed all of a sudden."

"A little. I've got a meeting with my financial advisor tomorrow. He's great, but figuring out what to do with money is one of my least favorite things."

She nods, humming thoughtfully. "That does sound terrible. But it could be worse. You could be unemployed, liable for fifteen-thousand-dollars worth of credit card debt your ex charged before he dumped you, with limited job prospects on the horizon."

I hand my card over to the bartender and turn to her with a scowl. "Your ex charged fifteen thousand dollars to your credit card?"

"Cards," she corrects. "He maxed them out. Now, even though I've never missed a payment, my credit score is in the shitter. That's why I haven't been able to get financing to buy a car."

"I'm beginning to see why you swore off dating for a while."

"Not for a while," she says, expression sobering. "Forever."

"Forever's an awful long time."

"Not really." She pushes her plate away and drops her napkin on top. "If I live to be eighty, I doubt I'll be interested in men for the last twenty years or so. That means I'm only swearing off dating for another thirty years. Not so long when you think about it. I mean, since I've been out on my own, it feels like time is streaking past at the speed of light. Trust me, when you're old, a year slips away so fast it makes your head swim."

"Ancient twenty-seven-year-old, thank you for blessing me with your wisdom from the far side of the veil of youth."

"You're welcome," she deadpans, and I smile even though I know she's not kidding, at least not completely.

The bartender returns with the check, which I sign.

"All right, old lady. You ready to go?" I finish off the last drink of my beer. In my younger days, the stress of an impending financial meeting, combined with the stress of the woman I'm falling for having zero interest in getting into a relationship, would have been enough to convince me to have another beer.

And another.

And another, until I was too passed out to feel anxious.

But I don't let myself go there anymore. I self-soothe with a long run instead of booze. Another way I'm proving to myself that I can be a responsible adult without the meds that make me feel sick to my stomach and slow me down on the ice. If I can handle adulting with ADHD, and an NHL career without melting down, I can handle a relationship on top of it.

It's taken me two weeks to decide Diana is worth the risk a girlfriend might pose to my ability to focus on the job. Surely if I keep applying steady, gentle, but insistent pressure in the form of mind-blowing orgasms and affectionate friendship, she'll come around to my way of thinking.

Or at least we'll both have fun while I'm giving romancing her my best shot.

I'm calculating whether there will be time for a quickie

when we get home—definitely, there's always time for the things that really matter—when Diana stops on the sidewalk outside the bar, tugging on my arm.

I glance down to find her focus glued to the window display across the street, where a family of mannequins in beach wear are showing off the latest swim fashions in artfully arranged sand.

I take one glance at the featureless white ovals where their faces should be and look away with a shudder.

"Let's go." I start toward the car, only to stop when Diana refuses to budge.

"I have to know," she says, dividing her attention between the nightmare creatures in the window and me. "Why mannequins? Why do they freak you out so much?"

"They just do," I say, the hairs at the back of my neck lifting.

"But why?" she presses. "It's called automatonophobia, you know. The fear of something that imitates a living being. I looked it up the other day." She cocks her head, eyes narrowing on the display. "Is it because they look sort of human, but aren't? Is that what bothers you?"

I swallow hard, refusing to have a phobia-induced meltdown in front of a woman I want to think of me as an adult with a magical unicorn penis, not a freak with a childlike fear. "No, I don't think that's it." I clear my throat before continuing in a relatively calm tone, "It started a long time ago. After something that happened when I was a kid."

"Tell me." She curls her fingers around my arm, pressing lightly into my bicep. "I mean, if it's not too personal."

Too personal...

For the first time in our brief acquaintance, Diana actually *wants* to know something personal. She wants to get in my head, figure out what makes me tick, and I understand the female mind well enough to realize that this is exactly what I want. It means she's interested, curious, tempted to get closer, no matter how often she's sworn her heart is a no-fly zone.

And damn if I'm going to let a phobia or anything else get in the way of satisfying her curiosity, or any other part of her that needs satisfying.

I take her hand and step to the edge of the curb, pressing the button on the crosswalk.

"Where are we going?" Her lips curve as she shoots me a wary look from the corners of her eyes. "We're not going into the store, are we?"

"We are. I think a visual aid will help you understand the origin story."

She bounces lightly on her toes. "Okay. I mean, as long as we have time."

"We've got time." I tighten my grip on her hand, enjoying the way it fits in mine, and that she's consented to public handholding—another good sign. "But you're going to owe me an embarrassing story in return."

"I have lots of those," she says with a nod. "And don't worry. If the mannequins try any funny stuff, I'll protect you."

It's clearly a joke, and I obviously don't need Diana to defend me from anyone—whether they're human or made of fiberglass—but something about the offer gets to me.

In the good way.

In the way that makes me want to pull her into my arms and kiss her until she melts. So I do. And even though we're at the edge of a crowded sidewalk next to a busier street, she doesn't push me away. She wraps her arms around my neck and kisses me back, her tongue dancing with mine.

By the time we come up for air, we've missed our first shot at crossing the street, so I hit the button a second time and reclaim her hand, knowing better than to start kissing her again if I want to make it across the street in the next half hour.

"What was that for?" She nudges my arm with her shoulder.

"For offering to be my princess in shining armor. Thank you."

She lifts her chin. "You're welcome. Though there's no reason I can't be a knight, you know."

"So, you're the knight, and I'm the prince in distress?"

She grins, the way I'd hoped she would. "Yes. Poor prince. You've needed a lot of protecting lately. First the killer mermaids, then a cranky pig, and now mannequins intent on world domination."

"Is that what they want? I've always been too scared to ask."

Diana nods. "That's what the forces of evil always want, right? I mean, deep down. They may have other superficial motives, but at the core, they all want to rule the world."

"Or burn it all down." I consider the question more seriously than I should. "Bad guys want to destroy everyone who isn't as miserable as they are, right? So ruling the world is just a step on the road to its eventual annihilation."

Her eyebrows do their thoughtful dance. "I think you might be right." She squeezes my hand. "I like talking to you."

"As much as fucking me?"

"Nearly," she says, clucking her tongue thoughtfully. "Very nearly."

Feeling like I've won some small but important battle, I step off the curb, hurrying across the road to the dragons waiting on the other side, ready to slay every one for a chance at this woman's heart.

CHAPTER THIRTEEN

DIANA

Inside the store, sticky-pink pop music bubbles from hidden speakers overhead and the conditioned air smells of Turkish delight, cherry candy, and wild roses, a sickeningly sweet combination that makes me suspect preteen girls are the store's target demographic. The walls covered in pink, purple, and retina-punching red confirm my hunch.

"You know one of the most traumatizing parts of being short?" I ask, following Tanner as he gives the mannequins a wide berth and moves deeper into the store.

"What?" He threads his way through racks of bubblegum-colored shirts, leggings, and mini-skirts.

"Being forced to wear clothes like this after I was old enough to drive a car because nothing in the women's section fit me. This is why pink and I got a divorce as soon as size zero became a thing at adult retail establishments."

Tanner hums beneath his breath. "That's a shame. You'd be pretty in pink."

I motion toward the display now twenty feet away. I'm uncomfortable with the compliment, the way I am with all compliments, especially from this person I'm trying hard not to think of as more than a fuck buddy. "So which one scares you more—the big daddy mannequin or the cute toddler mannequin wearing the bucket hat?" I wrinkle my nose at the pungent sparkle-sugar smell of the place. "I'm thinking the perfume display is the most terrifying thing in this joint, but I'm easily offended by bad smells."

"We can leave. My sister gets headaches in places like this. Wouldn't want to give you another migraine."

"Thanks, but I'm fine," I say, not missing the disappointment that flickers across his features. "And I have an idea. To help with the mannequins."

"Help how? Help destroy them before they destroy us?"

I grin. "Actually, I was thinking that you should show them who's dominant. Like with Wanda."

He hums dubiously. "Move the mannequin?"

"Exactly! Show them that you're the boss in this relationship and you're not going to take any more of their bullshit."

"You do realize that mannequins aren't alive, right?" He lowers his voice. "At least, not as far as they're willing to let on…"

"They don't have to be. It could still work. I didn't feel confident moving Wanda, either. I just made myself do it. I faked it until I maked it." I scrunch my nose and try again, forcing my fuzzy-feeling lips to enunciate. "Faked it until I made it. Sorry. I've had two beers, but I know what I mean. And you do, too, right?" I tap his furry forearm with eager fingers. "This could work. It's at least worth a shot."

"If I don't get arrested for messing with store property." He swivels to scope out the store over one shoulder and then the other. "Though it doesn't seem like anyone's interested in us, does it?"

I shake my head. "Nope. And they won't be. We're both too old and too large for their key demographic. You'll have the mannequins moved and be out the door before anyone gets around to asking us if we need a dressing room."

Tanner's lips press together, forming a white seam at the bottom of his paler-than-usual face.

"Think how good it would feel," I wheedle. "To know no one will ever be able to prank you with fiberglass humanoids ever again…"

His breath rushes out in a grunting huff. "Fine. I'll do it."

"Yes!" I pump my fist. "This is totally going to work! This is the day everything changes, Tanner. This is the day you kick this phobia's ass."

He rolls his eyes good-naturedly. "Maybe. But don't get your hopes up. The only thing I've had longer than a fear of mannequins is a hatred for pancakes."

I feel my eyes bulge comically wide. "What! How can you hate pancakes?"

"They're disgusting."

"What? No!" I shake my head and hold up my hands, fingers spread, needing to stop this madness before it goes any further. "They're amazing! And there are so many different flavors. You can't possibly hate them all. And maple syrup! Who hates maple syrup?"

He shrugs. "Not a fan. The more syrup you put on the pancake, the soggier and more disgusting it gets."

I brace a hand on the rack of glittery silver leggings next to me. "I may need to sit down. What other dark secrets are you hiding?"

He grins. "I'm trying to tell you."

Sighing in disappointment, I gesture for him to continue, though I'm not done with this pancake thing, not by a long shot. Pancakes are one of the world's most perfect foods, proof that even in the darkest night of the soul, the morning will come and it will be light and fluffy and drenched in syrup.

"So, I told you that sometimes I have trouble staying focused."

I nod, brow furrowing as I cross my arms.

"Well, it was even worse when I was a kid," he continues. "I spent most of elementary school bouncing off the walls or in the counselor's office playing with Legos while she gave me my tests aloud because I could only figure out the answers if I was doing something with my hands at the same time." He shakes his head. "Even back then, I was tight on the ice—hockey was so fast-paced I never had trouble focusing—but the rest of my life was pretty much chaos."

"I'm familiar with this chaos of which you speak," I say. "I have four siblings."

He laughs. "Yeah, well, I was crazy enough to make up for how calm my sisters were. I ripped through our house like a tornado, and if I didn't have someone riding my ass, staying on task was impossible. I wasn't a bad kid—I tried to follow the rules, but it was hard to exercise self-discipline when I couldn't remember what I was supposed to be doing from one minute to the next."

I bite my bottom lip, wincing in sympathy. "I can imagine. I'm sorry, Tanner. When we were talking the other day, I didn't realize…" I wave a hand vaguely toward the door and the house somewhere beyond. "I thought you were making an excuse for being addicted to your phone. I didn't realize this was something serious."

He shrugs as he slides his hands into the back pockets of his jeans. "No worries. I didn't give you much to go on. I've made a habit of not talking about it. I don't want it getting back to the guys on the team. Justin was already fucking with me about having untreated ADHD last year. I don't want the side-eye to get any worse."

"What?" My jaw drops. "That's awful! And not like him. I mean, he's a joker, but I've never known him to be mean."

"He wasn't," Tanner says. "He was fucking with the rookie. He doesn't know I actually have ADHD, or that I've been off my meds for three years. No one does except my family and my doctor, and I'd like to keep it that way."

"Oh..." I blink in surprise. "Of course. I won't tell anyone."

"Thanks. I don't want to get pressured to go back on drugs that make me feel dizzy and sick to my stomach."

"No pressure, but I've heard certain kinds of marijuana can help ADHD," I offer. "I could ask my pot doctor about it the next time I go in for a refill if you want."

"Maybe," he says, seeming more open to the suggestion than I expect him to be. "But I've really been doing okay. I had some trouble adjusting to the Badger system when I first joined the team—it's hard for me to establish new patterns—but eventually I hit on a way to keep the new strategies at the front of my mind. It's proven solid so far."

"What is it?" I ask, hurrying to add, "You don't have to tell me if you don't want. I'm just curious. I find things like this fascinating."

"Things like my misbehaving brain?" he asks, arching a brow.

"No!" I pause, lips pursing before I admit, "Well, yes, I guess. But not just you. All of us. It's wild, the ways we have to learn to work with our minds, to convince them to cooperate and keep us healthy and productive. Other animals don't have issues like that. They're born ready to do what it takes to stay alive. But humans..." I hold my thumbs up to show the divide between our lizard brain and our higher consciousness. "We're born divided and we have to figure out how to coax this stubborn, alien part of ourselves into being a friend instead of an enemy."

He studies me thoughtfully. "So normal people feel like that, too?"

I lean in, offering in a confidential whisper, "I hate to shatter your illusions, but I'm not normal. Not even close."

"You're normal enough." His fingers skim down my forearm until he captures my hand in his larger one, making my chest feel tighter and my breathing easier at the same time. "Anyway, you know what I mean."

I curl my fingers around his. "Yes, I think normal people feel like that, too. At least the ones I know. It's one of the universal truths about being human, and probably why we're our own worst enemies."

Tanner's lips curve mysteriously as he dips his head to my ear to ask in a husky voice, "Is this the right time to suggest that swearing off relationships—something humans need to survive, let alone thrive—could be an example of brain misbehavior?"

I narrow my eyes at him, but my glare doesn't reach its usual heat index. "No. This is the time to tell me why mannequins make you wet your pants."

His dimples pop. "It's more a be-sick-on-my-shoes feeling, but point taken." He nods toward the display. "So, I was a spacier than the average kid, and I wore my mother and sisters out trying to keep track of me. They would turn around for a second, and I'd be gone, off exploring, forgetting that I wasn't supposed to run off by myself."

He moves closer to the display with measured steps, as if sneaking up on a skittish and dangerous wild animal. "One day we were at the mall, just before Christmas. The place was packed, and Cheyenne was getting her ears pierced. I don't remember this part, but allegedly, Chey started freaking out, and Mom let go of my hand to keep Chey from slugging the teenage girl doing the piercings. When she turned back, I was gone."

"How old were you?" I follow him across the slick white tiles toward the mannequins as "Radioactive" begins to play over the sound system, lending an eerie vibe to our approach.

"Six." Tanner smiles at my soft gasp. "You would think a kid alone in the mall would be easy to find, but the security people looked for hours without any sign of me. I don't remember what I was doing that whole time, but I remember hearing the announcement that the store I was in was closing and suddenly realizing I was lost."

He pauses, his fingers clenching at his sides. "Sorry, I need a second."

I glance at the fiberglass statues a few feet away and back at Tanner, whose chest is rising and falling faster than it was before. "You don't have to do this. I'm not going to think any less of you if you want to bail."

"No." He stretches his neck to one side. "I've got this. Just need a second." He blows a breath out through pursed lips. "So I heard the announcement and decided I should leave the store and try to find my mom in the parking lot."

He points toward the ceiling, where bright fluorescents blast white light down onto the store. "I saw what I thought were streetlights through these two big doors at the back of the furniture department where I'd been playing, and I made a run for it. But it turned out to be a stock room. There were boxes stacked to the ceiling and all these shadowy corridors to creep down pretending to be a ninja turtle…" He grins, his dimples doing that dimple thing they do so well. "Needless to say, I lost track of time again."

"Who wouldn't? Did you avoid the evil Splinter and save your turtle brothers from certain doom?"

"I did. But by then, the lights were flicking off. I ran up and down the aisles, looking for someone to ask for help, and saw a group of people on the far side of the room. They were just silhouettes in the gray at that point, and by the time I made it over there, it was so dark I could barely see. It wasn't until I was on top of them that I realized they weren't people at all."

"They were mannequins," I supply, a chill shivering up my spine, lifting the hairs at the back of my neck.

"They were. Terrifying, faceless, creepy monsters. But I was too scared to keep wandering around in the dark. So I curled up in a ball and eventually cried myself to sleep." He cuts a glance to his left, where the dad mannequin is nearly close enough to touch. "An older man who worked in the stock room found me the next morning, but he only spoke Spanish, so it took a while for me to communicate how much I needed to get away from the mannequins."

I lay a hand on his arm, but he doesn't flex, proving he's truly in deep distress. "You poor thing."

"My poor mom. She spent the night at the police station with my sisters. The cops thought some child molester had snatched me out of the mall."

I hook my elbow through his. "Want to get out of here? Maybe this isn't worth it, after all."

He stands his ground. "Huh-uh. I'm not going to be that guy."

"What guy?"

"The punch line in a joke you tell your girlfriends guy."

I step away, my arm sliding free as I turn to face him. "You're my friend, not a punch line, and you're clearly upset, which isn't the kind of thing I find amusing. People getting hurt or feeling scared doesn't hit me in the funny bone. I'm not an asshole."

"I know you're not." He glances up. "But you're stubborn. You know why I have to do this."

"I do." I cant my head to the side with a sigh. "Well, is there anything I can do to help? Hold your hand maybe?"

"Just be here. And give me a countdown?" His fingers

flutter at his sides, like an Olympic swimmer waiting for the gun to send him diving into the water.

"All right. On the count of three. One..." I take a deep breath, willing peace his way. "Two..." I cross my fingers, both sets. "Three!"

Moving stiffly, but steadily, Tanner reaches out, grabbing the dad mannequin around the waist and lifting him into the air. A moment later, he's crossed to the other side of the platform and set Dad down by the plastic dog, before fetching the tween mannequin, who he arranges beside her toddler brother. A few minutes later and he's reinvented the display, and the shiny plastic people look like they're having more fun on the beach than they were before.

"I love it!" I exclaim in a whisper, clapping my hands. "How do you feel?"

"Okay." Tanner exhales sharply. "Good actually. Maybe I should move them some more? Really break through the crazy once and for all?"

I glance over my shoulder, on the lookout for store employees coming to chastise us, but there still isn't anyone in sight.

"I think there's another way." I take his hand and pull him over to where the mom mannequin is leaning against the surfboard at the edge of the display. "Give her a hug."

He snorts. "What?"

"Give her a hug." I lay my hands on his upper arms from behind. "Go for it. I'll be right here."

"You want me to hug this mannequin?"

"Yes." I step in, pressing my front to his back. "Just concentrate on my boobs pressing against you and you'll be just fine."

He laughs. "You're a mind reader, aren't you?"

"Maybe a little." I go up on tiptoe, letting my lips brush

against his neck as I whisper, "Come on, Tanner. Do it. And walk out of this store a free man."

"You're very committed to fixing me, Daniels."

"You don't need fixing," I say, because it's the truth. "You're good just the way you are."

Tanner tenses, and for a second I think he's going to pull away. But instead, he reaches out, wraps his arms around Mom Mannequin, and draws her close.

For several long moments, we stand in silence, with Tanner's arms around the mannequin and my arms around him. And I'm sure anyone watching would think we're out of our minds or high on reality-altering drugs, but it's one of the sweeter moments I've shared with another human being. Helping someone face their fears is special. It doesn't matter if it's the fear of terrorists, or a nuke hitting the west coast, or a childhood-trauma-inspired fear of mannequins—fear is fear.

And fear is the opposite of love, I realize as Tanner whispers, "It's good. For real. I'm not freaked out anymore," and a cozy, wonderful, warm feeling fills my chest.

By the time it becomes clear that I've waded into deeper emotional waters than I expected to encounter during a move-the-mannequin mission, Tanner turns, pulls me into his arms, and kisses me with enough heat to melt every scented candle in this stinky store.

My blood ignites, and my head swims, and I suddenly feel like I'm standing at the edge of a cliff watching the ocean prove that there are some things in the world that never get old or jaded or tired. Some things that are strong enough and grown-up enough to say they're up for forever and understand exactly what they're promising.

Before I can process this information—or achieve the level of terror such epically romantic thoughts should inspire

—a nasal voice sounds from a few feet away. "Hey! You two! You can't do that in here. This is a family store!"

Tanner and I separate, breath rushing out in surprise. I turn to see a girl in a hot-pink tube dress and black cat-eye glasses glaring at us from the T-shirt table. She meets my gaze for an irritated second before glancing past me, her eyes widening. "What happened to the display?" she asks, pink lips parting in dismay. "Did you do that?"

"Run," Tanner murmurs, taking my hand. "Now."

"Hey, come back!" the sales associate shouts after us as we dash for the exit, hurrying out into the warm summer air, accompanied by the intro music from "Under Pressure" blasting from the speakers.

CHAPTER FOURTEEN

From the Skype Log of Tanner Nowicki
and Cheyenne Nowicki

CHEYENNE: Hey doofus, where's my pig? You promised me Wanda in a cute outfit. Everyone in the shop is jonesing for new pig pics. We're making a pet collage on the back of the office door.

TANNER: Strapped for entertainment over there, huh?

CHEYENNE: You bet your sweet ass we are. There's nothing to do on base but drink, drink and play pool, or drink and sleep with people you're not supposed to sleep with.

TANNER: Why not go off base?

Cheyenne: I'm working too much. It's a disease. And I hate shopping for knockoff purses, which is all my friends here want to do.

Cute pig photos are my only source of frivolous entertainment.

Tanner: Sorry, it slipped my mind. I forgot to put it on the list, and Wanda's already asleep. But I'll write it down right now so I won't forget next time.

Cheyenne: No worries. How's the list thing going, by the way?

Tanner: Good.

Cheyenne: Just good? Could I get a little more info? You know Mom stresses and then likes to call me and leave long, rambling, worried messages.

Tanner: That's because Mom is a meddler who thinks pills are magic.

Cheyenne: Well, pills can be magic. Sort of. Sometimes.

And there's no shame in needing them, Tanner. It's no different than a diabetic needing insulin shots.

TANNER: Except that I'm a professional athlete, and I can't afford to have a dizzy spell at the wrong time. My career would be over.

CHEYENNE: You could try different meds.
There are a lot of options these days.

TANNER: Yeah, I heard tonight marijuana was a thing for ADHD. Who knew?

CHEYENNE: Are you smoking in my house?!

TANNER: *laughter* No, I'm not. Relax.

CHEYENNE: I mean, if you need it for medical purposes, that's fine, but you have to hide it before I get home and accidentally touch it. I had a friend who tested positive on a drug screening just from being in the same room as someone who had a smoked a joint the day before.

TANNER: I doubt the truth of that story, but I hear you.

CHEYENNE: Do you? For real?

TANNER: Yes, Chey. I'm actually a fully-grown adult person who takes things seriously these days. I'm meeting with my financial manager tomorrow, and tonight over dinner I was discussing whether I would ever want to be a stay-at-home dad.

CHEYENNE: Oh my God, the thought of you as a father is terrifying.

TANNER: Thanks for the vote of confidence.

CHEYENNE: I didn't mean it like that! You'll be a great dad. I just meant knowing you're old enough to talk about stuff like that reminds me how ancient I am. I should start trying to find someone I have permission to sleep with and get knocked up. Or maybe get married and then get knocked up, though, with the crazy divorce rate in my line of work, it's probably better to go straight to the kid and custody arrangements and forgo the brief, foolish interlude of hope and romance.

TANNER: It doesn't have to fall apart.
Some people make hope and romance work for the long haul.

CHEYENNE: Ugh, you're such a romantic. You always have been.
Even when you were a baby, crushing on that little girl who lived down the street. You can't be trusted to see the world as it really is.

TANNER: Or maybe your pessimism is keeping you from opening yourself up to a healthy relationship. Ever think about that?

CHEYENNE: Stop sounding reasonable and smart. It makes me uncomfortable.

TANNER: *laughs*

CHEYENNE: So how are things on your dating front? Have you abandoned your pattern of serial monogamy and taken advantage of your newfound fame to score mad lady-tail?

TANNER: I'm not really into mad lady-tail.
Tail without feelings isn't my thing. I like quality, not quantity.

CHEYENNE: Aw, look at your face right now! You're so cute!
Oh my God, are you in love? You're in love, aren't you?

TANNER: *eye roll* I'm not in love.

CHEYENNE: Oh yes you are. You're blushing bright red like a big, adorable doofus! Who is it? How long have you been dating? And why didn't you say anything before now? You know I need gossip to ease my loneliness.

TANNER: I'm not dating anyone. We're just hanging out, and it's only been a couple weeks so…

CHEYENNE: That's fast. But when you know, you know, right?

TANNER: Are you the same person who just said hope and romance are dead?

CHEYENNE: Not dead. Just foolish. For me. But not for you!
Not to give you a big head, baby brother, but you're a total catch. Sweet, successful, hard working, and easy on the eyes—as long as you like blond guys with creepy golden facial hair.

TANNER: Thanks. I appreciate the vote of confidence, but it's too soon to put a label on anything. But she is special. She got me to hug a mannequin tonight.

CHEYENNE: What? Holy shit! Are you for real?

TANNER: For real. And it wasn't bad. It was liberating, actually.

CHEYENNE: Get the fuck out. Where is my baby brother?
What did you do to him, you evil cyborg replacement person?

TANNER: *laughs*

CHEYENNE: I'm talking to an alien virus that's using my brother's body as a host, aren't I? Because there is no way my actual real life brother would ever touch a mannequin, let alone hug one.

TANNER: What can I say?
I think this is the summer I leave that stupid shit behind.

CHEYENNE: Wow.
Do you think this girl can help me get over my fear of bugs, too?
Every time I have to sweep the hangar when the bugs are swarming, I get so worked up I sweat through my uniform and Guzman and Fowler make fun of me for a solid twenty-four hours after.

TANNER: Maybe. Though, that reminds me, Wanda didn't like Diana too much at first. She actually bit her.

CHEYENNE: Oh shit, no! Bad pig! Tell Diana I'm so, so sorry!

TANNER: It's okay. We're working on behavior adjustments, and so far Wanda seems to be coming around. At least she's not hiding behind doors and jumping out to scare Diana anymore.

CHEYENNE: Diana, huh? The new roommate is your new squeeze, isn't she?

Ha! I knew it! I knew you couldn't cohabitate with a woman without banging her. But your captain is going to have your ass, right? That's against team rules, isn't it? Like if I decided to bang someone in my chain of command?

TANNER: Except that I won't lose a stripe or wreck my career.

I'll just have some of the team pissed at me until they realize I know how to treat people I care about.

CHEYENNE: AW!!! You are in love! I knew it!

TANNER: Oh, shut up! And keep your voice down!

She's just down the hall, and the last time I checked, she had ears.

CHEYENNE: Oh good, I like people with ears.

I can't wait to meet her! And tell her thank-you for putting up with my badly behaved pig and my weirdo brother. Maybe you could thank her for me. And apologize for Wanda. I should have done a better job socializing her with strangers when she was a baby. That's totally my bad.

TANNER: Will do. Chat same time next week?

CHEYENNE: Sounds good. And keep an eye on the mail

between now and then. I ordered something adorable for Wanda. You should put it on her before you walk her next time. It'll be a great conversation starter.

TANNER: I'm afraid to ask. This is your way of continuing to embarrass me even though you're thousands of miles away, isn't it?

CHEYENNE: Mortification and mockery are how I show my love, baby brother.
   Take care of yourself, okay? And give Mom a call.

TANNER: I will.

CHEYENNE: All right. I miss you.

TANNER: I miss you, too. Can't wait until you're home safe.

CHEYENNE: Ditto.

CHAPTER FIFTEEN

DIANA

It's a gorgeous day for a drive, with the sun shining in the blue, blue sky and Mount Hood majestic in the distance, wearing its tiny, summer-sized snowcap. A part of me wants to keep driving, just head off into the wilderness and get lost for a week or two, but that's the fear talking.

That's the voice in my head that assures me that if I fuck up this interview, I'll have to get a job flipping burgers or scooping ice cream to make ends meet, and nearly a decade of dedication to my craft will have all been for nothing. I'll be right back where I started when I got my first job sophomore year of high school, waiting tables at Bill's Taco Palace. Except this time around I'll have to find a way to make a minimum wage job stretch to cover my room and board since I won't be shacking up with my parents.

"No way, Daniels. you are going to ace this interview," I murmur to my reflection as I smooth on a coat of lipstick and check my hair in the parking lot of Good Timber's new St. Johns location, next to several trendy home goods stores and a gourmet cheese shop. "You look good, your portfolio looks good, and these guys are down to earth people who are hoping you're the one they're looking for so they can stop looking and get back to making beer and drinking beer and thinking up fun slogans for beer T-shirts."

I hold my own gaze for a long moment, waiting until the anxiety tightening the edges of my eyes relaxes and I look like a calm, collected, only slightly crazy professional creative person. My outfit is perfect this time—a short white cotton sundress covered with brightly colored flowers, worn over a pair of suit pants made of jeans fabric, and cowgirl boots. I look like a girl who likes to work hard and think whimsical, publicity-friendly thoughts, but isn't too uptight to enjoy a beer at the end of the day.

I'm as ready as I'll ever be, so it's time to get in there and knock this interview out of the park.

I swing out into the day, fetch my battered antique portfolio case from the trunk of Laura's car—thankful for her willingness to let Brendan shuttle her to and from work today—and head for the tinted glass doors beneath a row of carved wooden animal heads adorning the Good Timber entrance. Inside, the same dim, middle-of-an-enchanted-forest vibe I experienced at the downtown location reigns, making me feel even more at home.

There are still a few workers laying tile, and the large wall on my right displays a half-finished mural of an owl taking flight, but the same graceful totem poles are already installed throughout the dining room, and the bar is a roughly carved chunk of redwood that is flat-out stunning. I can already tell that this space is going to be even lovelier than the flagship bar, as well as a more hangout-friendly location. In addition to the bar and dining areas, there's a courtyard in the back, ringed by ivy-covered walls.

It's from the courtyard that a tall, dark-haired man in jeans and a Good Timber T-shirt emerges, walking toward me with a smile. "Diana?"

I nod and hold out an only slightly trembling hand. "Jax?"

"That's me," he says, displaying almost alarmingly white teeth as he takes my hand and gives it a firm squeeze. "So glad you could come chat today."

"Me, too. It's great to see the new place." I gesture to the room at large. "I love everything you've got going on here."

"Awesome. Because we love your work." He motions for me to follow him to the back of the restaurant. "My partners are out on the patio. Come meet them, and we can talk about what we're looking for. Steve, our current PR guy, is here, too, so he can answer any creative questions you might have. The rest of us are beer makers and money managers, so we're useless for anything except saying we love a concept or don't love it just yet."

I smile as I fall in beside him, liking that he doesn't shorten his long stride for me. "I wouldn't call that useless. Beer making and money managing are arts of their own."

"Thanks. I'll have to get you to talk to my mother next time she's in town. She thinks I'm wasting my life getting people drunk."

"Mothers are tricky like that sometimes," I say vaguely, not wanting to get too familiar.

But it's hard. Jax is easy to talk to, and his business partners for this location—Kyle and Kevin—are the cutest hipster couple I've ever met. They have matching well-trimmed beards and beanie caps, and plaid shirts that are clearly trying to pull off a lumberjack vibe but are too crisply pressed and decorated with eclectic buttons to be anything other than adorable. Steve is super nice, too—a tall, thin, serious-looking man in his thirties with expressive hands who tells surprisingly funny jokes.

We talk for the better part of an hour. The men explain how they want Good Timber to be a culture, a way of life, a family more than a brand. I chat with them about my work with the National Park Service, and how so much of what I did, aside from taking pretty pictures, was keeping the public informed about the gift they'd been given when the parks were created and building a feeling of good will and gratitude.

"Our goal was that every time you see a National Park sign, you should feel warm, cozy, and thankful inside," I explain. "And maybe a little nostalgic, for the good old days of camping and hiking with your family when you were a kid."

Jax nods. "I get that."

"I think you succeeded," Steve adds. "I started donating to the parks just two years ago, largely because of your publicity efforts. Before that, the parks were one of those things I didn't think about as often as I should, considering how much time my wife and I spend outdoors."

"Well, it wasn't just my effort," I hurry to clarify. "I was one of the moving parts. But it was rewarding work. And I think we could do something similar with Good Timber."

We chat for another twenty minutes, and then Jax leaves to take a phone call, only to return a few moments later with a beer sampler flight from the bar.

As he sets it at the center of the table, Kevin says, "I completely agree." Kyle adds, "Me, too," and Steve smiles and gives a thumbs-up.

I blink, turning to watch Jax as he settles into his seat beside me. "Did I miss something?"

"Not at all," he says. "Just wanted to see if you would like to try some of the new brews we'll be introducing this fall. We're going to offer you the job, so we thought you might want to try the product first. See if you're still excited to take us on after you've tasted the Pumpkin Sour, which we're warning our patrons is a bit of an acquired taste."

My grin explodes across my cheeks, leaving me no time to talk my face into playing it cool. "Really? I've got the job?"

"If you want it," Jax says. "You had the best interview, and we could really use some feminine energy around here. Since our other partner left to start a brewery in Washington, we've been more out of balance than usual."

"I would love to be the feminine energy," I say, fighting to keep from bouncing up and down in my chair. "And I would love the job. Thank you so, so much. I can't wait to get to work!"

We celebrate with a tasting of five delicious beers—even the Pumpkin Sour is phenomenal, and I usually can't stand anything pumpkin flavored—and by the time I head for the door, I've worked up an unexpected buzz. If I'd eaten lunch, I would be fine, but I was too nervous to eat before the interview. Now, I should probably give myself an hour or two—and a meal—before I drive Laura's car back to my brother's house.

Acting on the spur of the moment, I text Tanner, *Want to meet me in St. John's near the new Good Timber location? And let me treat you to dinner? Looks like they've got a few places to choose from. Mexican, a bistro type place, a Brazilian steakhouse...*

After only a moment, he responds. *I'll be there in five. Just got done at the gym, so I'm not far. I'm assuming this means the interview went well?*

Yeah, pretty well, I text back, grinning like a loon as I hit caps lock and add, *BECAUSE THEY OFFERED ME THE FUCKING JOB AND I FUCKING TOOK IT, MOTHERFUCKER!!!*

Congratulations!!! Tanner responds. *That's amazing news! I'm so happy for you. I knew you'd rock that interview. You're exactly the kind of smart, creative, crazy person they need around there.*

My thumbs hover over the keypad as I bite my lip and

try to think of something more eloquent to say than "thanks for helping me get the interview." But my brain is beer and post-interview-stress-release fuzzy, so I just tap out, *Can't wait to buy you a beer. Thanks so much for your help. It's going to be so wonderful to be an employed member of the populace again.*

My pleasure, Pixie. Always happy to help. See you soon. He sends a beer emoji and a confetti emoji, and I continue to smile as I roll my eyes.

"Such a dork with the emojis," I mutter as I wander toward the shops and restaurants farther down the street, sending him a smiling poop, a happy monster, and a little alien video game creature jumping up and down.

I usually won't touch an emoji with a ten-foot pole, but I'm a little tipsy and I know they'll make Tanner laugh.

And I like making him laugh.

I like it a lot. I like it so much it should be scaring the shit out of me. I know this even before he sends back a unicorn and an eggplant, making me laugh so hard I have to stop to lean against the brick wall of the building next to me and catch my breath.

I'm still there, giggling and blushing and making a spectacle of myself, when a familiar silhouette emerges from the fancy home goods store just ahead.

It's the kind of place where you can buy fine china with limited edition patterns, hand-carved chairs from Denmark, and sinfully soft Egyptian cotton napkins dyed such beautiful colors it seems a shame to use them to wipe spaghetti sauce from the corners of your mouth. In other words, it's the kind of place I never set foot in. Not because I don't love beautiful things, but because I've moved so much for work that I've never had time to decorate. And then there's the matter of having little or no disposable income. My money goes right back into lenses, flash attachments, and bigger, badder hard drives to handle the processing of massive image files.

But in my secret heart of hearts, I've harbored fine china type wishes. Or at least fancy plate type wishes. I've always thought I would like to buy one place setting of several different patterns, so I would always have something that fit my present state of mind and meal.

Japanese blue calligraphy with intricate flowers around the rim for Sunday morning breakfast, peacocks waving flags to spruce up a lunchtime salad, and hand-painted woodland creatures for afternoon fruit and nut snacks or evenings when a boiled egg, slices of avocado, and a few pickles are as fancy as I can bring myself to get with dinner.

Suffice it to say, I've thought enough about these kinds of things to experience a pang of longing when I walk by a window display featuring carefully chosen combinations of plates and bowls artfully arranged on a table. But that pang is nothing compared to the marrow-deep flash of agony that ricochets through my bones as I realize who that familiar silhouette belongs to.

It's Sam—my Sam, the only man who ever made me think that maybe the whole "happily ever after" thing wasn't a complete crock of shit after all—and he's not alone.

Beside him, dressed in a sky-blue linen sundress with birds taking wing near the hem, is Madeline. Madeline of the lily-white complexion, bee-stung red lips, and glossy black hair she keeps tied back in a crisp ribbon like a modern day, all-grown-up Snow White. In addition to the lovely face, Madeline has curves for miles, tiny feet that look ridiculously precious in kitten-heel pumps, and a big, sexy brain that does important work for refugees in crisis. She's an attorney at a non-profit who spends her spare time backpacking in exotic locales, somehow managing to remain flawlessly elegant and gorgeous even after sweating it up in the jungles of South America for the better part of a week.

I know this about Madeline because I am one of those weak-willed human beings who Googles her ex just to slice open a pain vein and sob about how much it hurts. At least once every few months or so, I drink too much wine, misplace my instinct of self-preservation, and end up cruising through Sam's most recent social media posts, scanning shots of him and Madeline hamming it up in selfies from the top of a mountain they've climbed, cuddling near the fireplace at a friend's party, or laughing adorably over happy hour beverages and karaoke.

Stalking was how I found out Sam and Madeline were engaged in the first place. How I learned that the ring was of a moderate size—Sam's a travel writer and far richer in adventures and tall tales than cold, hard cash—but exceeding loveliness. It's an antique, with a rose diamond as elegant and flawless as Madeline herself.

I can see the ring now. My gaze locks on it, staring it down like the barrel of a gun aimed in my direction, unable to tear my eyes away even when Sam draws to an abrupt halt outside the store and says in an uncomfortably stunned tone, "Diana? What a surprise seeing you here."

With panic gripping my throat, I look away from the evidence of just how completely Sam has moved on from that endless summer we shared two years ago, and up to meet his eyes. The moment my gaze crashes into his baby blues, my heart shrivels into a tiny, sad raisin, lying dehydrated in a dusty corner of a kitchen someone forgot to sweep.

It is something that was once good, then decent, and now would be better off in the trash. But no one cares enough to bother. My desiccated heart is so wretchedly beneath notice that it can't even be properly thrown away.

The metaphor is strained, but I can't help it. That's where my thoughts go and where they stay—in the sad kitchen with the pathetic, dusty, abandoned raisin—as my lips curve and I say, "Hey, Sam! Nice to see you. Congratulations on your engagement!"

Madeline, who has stood silently smiling—warmly, if a bit uncomfortably—says, "Thank you," at the same moment Sam asks, "How did you know?"

I realize that I've made a serious lapse—always a bad idea to forget what you've learned cyber-stalking and what you've been told in real life—and scramble to figure out a way I could have found out about Sam's engagement that would leave my dignity intact. But we have no friends in common, no intersections in our work, and I seriously doubt Madeline went to the effort to have their engagement announced in the paper. She's too busy saving refugee children and exploring the world to waste time crowing about her upcoming nuptials.

I open my mouth to babble something about "hearing it around somewhere" when I'm cut off by an arm wrapping around my waist and a deep voice that says, "Sorry to keep you waiting, beautiful."

I look up into Tanner's handsome face, my raisin heart plumping at the warmth in his eyes. "No worries." I sag against him. "It's fine."

"It's not fine, and it won't happen again." He leans down, capturing my lips in a long, sweet, thorough kiss that makes my shriveled heart swell to its full size, plus a little extra plumpness from pure gratitude.

I have no idea how he knew I needed this kiss, this rescue, but I'm so grateful for it. And I'm so thankful to have someone to lean on as the kiss ends and I turn back to Sam and Madeline with a rush of breath. "Sorry. Tanner, this is Sam and…" I furrow my brow, pretending to rack my brain and come up empty. "I'm sorry, but I don't think we've—"

"Madeline," she pipes up, her Snow White face beaming brightly as she glances from me to Tanner. "Madeline Sparks. And you're Tanner Nowicki. I'm a huge Badgers fan. Sam and I were at the first game you played last year."

Tanner laughs. "Sorry about that. Took me a few games to hit my stride."

"No!" Madeline shakes her head emphatically. "You were great! And you just kept getting better as the season went on. I hope you're going to be in Portland again this year."

"I am," Tanner confirms. "Love this city, and Badger fans are the best."

Sam chuckles, a sarcastic sound that's unlike him. Or at least, it's unlike the Sam I used to know, the one who had such a wide-open heart that he could find wonder in the smallest things. "I don't know about that. We're a restrained crew compared to the animals north of the border. I'm from Canada, where hockey is something you bleed for, not just an evening's entertainment. Right, Diana?"

I nod in Canadian solidarity—another great thing about Sam, he always understood and enthusiastically supported my Canadian pride. "Absolutely. But I confess it's nice to go to a game without having to watch grown men burst into tears when their team doesn't make the playoffs."

"I guess." The skin at the sides of Sam's eyes wrinkles in that way that used to make me melt. "Though you have to respect their passion."

I swallow hard, wishing he hadn't said that word. I don't want to think about passion right now, not with the man I used to love standing so close I can smell his wheat berry cologne mixing with his fiancée's lighter, sweeter perfume, and the man I'm trying to have uncomplicated sex with rubbing his palm up and down my side, from my waist to the curve of my hip and back again. I feel trapped between the tragic past and the impossible present, and the pressure is squeezing my brain like a stress ball.

Before I can blurt out something stupid or make a break for the Mexican restaurant across the street to drown my angst in an extra large frozen margarita, Tanner comes to the rescue again. "Hate to cut hockey talk short, but we've got reservations. Nice meeting you Sam, Madeline." He nods to each of them in turn before guiding me around the happy couple.

"Nice to meet you, too!" Madeline says, fluttering slim fingers.

"Absolutely," Sam agrees. "See you around."

Good God, I hope not, I think even as I echo, "See you."

But I don't want to see him. Ever. If I never see Sam's sky-blue eyes, adorably shaggy mop of brown curls, or lean, athletic hiker's body again, I'll count myself a lucky woman. Being close to him is like looking at faded pictures from my childhood, except a thousand times worse.

Childhood is something that everyone has to mourn, no matter how rich or fabulous or lucky they are. We all have to let go of those innocent days when life held so many possibilities and the future was nothing but clean sheets of paper, a rainbow of sharply pointed pencils, and dreams enough to fill each page with unique and beautiful things.

But true love is different. True love is something that some people get to hold onto, a dream they get to keep dreaming without ever waking up.

"You okay?" Tanner asks softly.

"Fine," I lie. "How did you know?"

"That Sam was your ex? The one who got away?" Tanner asks. When I nod, he continues, "You had that look on your face."

"The 'I just ran into someone I used to love and I want to

throw up' look?" I groan. "Great. And here I was hoping I'd managed to hide it."

"You were fine. He looked uncomfortable, too." He puts his arm around my shoulders, hugging me closer. "Madeline was the only one who wasn't on the verge of losing her lunch. She seems nice. I mean, if you like that sort of woman."

I glare up at him. "What sort? The sexy grown-up Disney princess with big boobs and a bigger brain and a relentlessly sunny disposition?"

His lips curve. "The sort that isn't you, clearly the superior specimen in every way."

I sigh, even as my heart starts plumping up with happiness again. "You're such a liar. She's beautiful and successful and seemingly very nice."

"But she's not a beach pixie. Once you've had one of those, I don't see how you could ever be happy with anything else."

I turn to face him under the awning of a French restaurant advertising crispy peppered lamb shoulder as the night's special. "You don't have to flatter me, Tanner. I'm fine. Sam and I have been broken up for a long time. It's no big deal. It was just…unexpected, running into him like that. That's all."

"I'm not flattering you." Tanner's green eyes glitter with anger and something else I can't quite pin down. "And Sam is a fuckwit idiot loser with stupid hair."

My grin comes in fast and sudden, cracking through the tension tightening my jaw. "No, he isn't. But thank you."

"You're welcome." He nods his head toward the restaurant. "French good?"

"French is lovely." I push onto my toes to kiss his freshly shaved cheek. "Thank you, unicorn."

"Unicorn cock, you mean," he says, wrapping his arm around my waist and drawing me closer.

I shake my head. "No, just unicorn. It's more than your dick that's special. You seem to be in possession of an encouraging, thoughtful, magical personality as well, you lucky bastard."

He smiles, and his eyes dance mischievously in the fading evening light. "Why, Miss Daniels, that may be the nicest thing you've ever said to me."

"Don't let it go to your head. Either one of them," I caution in my cranky old lady voice, the one I like to practice so I'll be ready when I'm an ancient spinster yelling at the neighborhood kids to get off my lawn.

But Tanner only laughs and kisses me again, a long, panty-melting kiss that leaves me feeling grateful to the coed who stole my deposit and ran off to Mexico. What would I have done without this man?

This sexy, silly, sensitive man who makes me wish…

I don't let the thought find its tail end. There's no room for that kind of wishing in my life—seeing Sam has reminded me what it feels like to lose someone who makes you feel irreplaceable, how it guts you like a fresh kill to see the person you thought was your forever planning a life with someone else.

I don't think I could survive that a second time. I know I couldn't.

That's why this has to stay sex and nothing more.

"We're just fucking," I whisper against Tanner's lips. "Don't take this too seriously, Muscle Boy."

"Oh, shut up and get your ass inside." Tanner slaps me softly on both ass cheeks, making my jaw drop.

"What was that for?" I ask indignantly.

"Let's eat and toast your new job before you start reminding me not to fall in love with you, okay?" he says, reaching to open the door. "I'm hungry, and I want to be happy with you first."

I cross my arms and scowl up at him. "Fine."

He smiles. "You're good to me."

I duck into the restaurant beneath his arm, catching a glimpse of Sam and Madeline crossing the street at the end of the block. Madeline is motioning toward yet another fancy home goods store, while Sam presses a kiss to the top of her glossy head. The sight of it hurts, but it doesn't hurt like a shriveled up raisin on a neglected kitchen floor.

In fact, it only aches softly, like a mostly-healed bruise.

And the reason for that muted ache is the man slipping into the restaurant behind me, his hand light at the small of my back, making me feel unreasonably adored.

CHAPTER SIXTEEN

TANNER

After dinner, I follow Diana to her brother's place, where she drops off Laura's car before slipping quietly down the driveway and into mine. I take her home, where the moment I shift the car into park, I lean over to steal a long, slow, red-wine-and-dark-chocolate-cake-flavored kiss. I kiss her on the way up the porch steps and into the house and across the kitchen as I scoop out food for Wanda and promise to walk her as soon as I've taken care of something very important.

"And what's that?" Diana asks, her breath catching as I draw her close.

"You, Daniels. I'm going to take care of you." And then I kiss her again, keeping her lips too busy to say any of things I can't stand for her to say right now. I don't want more warnings to guard my heart or reminders to keep her at arm's length.

I don't want her at arm's length. I want her tight against me, her breath in my mouth, her heartbeat echoing in my chest, her skin hot against mine. I want her time and attention, her laughter and tears, her smartass jokes and thoughtful touches and way of saying my name like she's got a secret and can't wait to share it with me. Whatever crazy thing she's going to say next, I want to be the first person to hear it, and when she goes to sleep, I want to be the last thing she touches before we turn out the light.

Because I'm falling in love with her, faster and deeper with every passing day, and it's too late for warnings to do a damn bit of good.

It was too late that first night on the beach, when she was still half fairy tale and moonlight. She slipped under my skin with her tinkle of a laugh and lodged herself there with the soft confession of how much she'd needed to be touched that night.

Now, I need to be touched by her every night, every afternoon, every moment I can steal, every second I can hold her close and make her feel so good she forgets all the reasons she's supposed to push me away.

I kiss her as I scoop her into my arms and head for my bedroom, and I'm still kissing her long minutes later after I've stripped away her clothes and mine. And then she's beneath me, welcoming me in as I push forward, leaving the darkness of my shadowed bedroom behind for the light that floods through me every time I make love to this woman.

It's not just fucking with Diana. It never has been, but tonight I don't try to hide how much this means. How much she means.

I don't take her hard or fast. I don't whisper dirty things into her ear or make wicked promises I intend to keep. I go slow, gliding in and out of her tight heat until rhythm gives way to conversation, until I'm confessing my sins with every advance and retreat, every breath gasped in between kisses, every groan as her nails dig into my ass, pulling me closer.

Forgive me, Diana, for I have sinned.

I've fallen in love with you, and I live to be inside you, beside you, as close as I can get.

Like this...

And this...

And this, oh God, this...

Can't you feel it? Can't you feel how good it is, Beach Pixie? My beautiful, crazy, perfect girl who makes me feel and feel and feel—God, the things you make me feel.

"Why?" she whispers, voice catching as we race faster toward the inevitable fall. "Why?"

"Because you're beautiful," I say, not pretending to misunderstand her. "Every part of you."

"But you barely know me." A tear slips down her cheek, which I kiss away.

"Lies." I slip a hand between us, rubbing her clit in firm circles as my cock strokes deeper. "I know you. And you know me. And there's no reason to be afraid. I'm never going to hurt you."

"Don't make promises you can't keep."

"I don't." My teeth dig into my bottom lip as I fight to keep from falling until I feel her go. "Now shut up and come for me, psycho."

"You're psycho," she says, but her lips curve and she pulls me closer, clinging to my shoulders as her words become a moan. "Oh yes. Yes, I'm so close. So close."

"And I'm going to get you closer, baby." My balls are swollen and heavy, and the need to come is so powerful I could go at any second, but I need her release first.

I need her pleasure as much as I need my own. More, because in that undefended moment when she's shot through with bliss, Diana is no longer a woman with a painful past and a suspicious eye narrowed at the future. When she comes for me, on me, with my body buried deep inside hers, she is a goddess—a fearless, shining, magical creature who takes my breath away with her beauty.

This time when she arches beneath me, her features twisting as her release takes her over, I fall a little harder, the way I do every time I make her mine, and then I come. I come so hard I spiral out of my skin, taking up orbit around a distant star before landing back in my body just as Diana begins to wiggle beneath me, the way she does when "you feel nicely heavy on top of me" becomes "you're starting to crush me, dude, roll over."

I rock onto my back, drawing her on top of me as I do because I'm not ready for one to become two just yet. "Good?" I ask.

She makes a *phfft,* so-much-better-than-good sound that makes me smile.

I sigh as I pat her bare ass. "I love making you come. It's my favorite hobby."

"Tanner, we should stop this." She props up on one arm, digging her finger and thumb into the corners of her closed eyes. "We really should. Yes, the sex is crazy good, but I don't want either of us to get hurt, and I don't—"

"No more talking. Not tonight." I stroke her hair until she finally relaxes onto my chest. "Be a quiet, snuggly beach pixie, not a worrying about things that don't need worrying about beach pixie."

She grumbles something I can't understand but remains where she is, her cheek warm on my skin and her fingers tracing the curve of my bicep, back and forth, back and forth, until she finally goes still.

A moment later, her soft snuffle of a snore fills the room, a sound as incongruously obnoxious and adorable as the woman herself.

I smile. Looks like she's sleeping over in my bed for the first time. It's a small victory, but a victory nevertheless.

"I'll take it," I whisper to the fan whirring overhead, letting myself drift off with a smile on my face, silently apologizing to Wanda for missing our nightly walk.

But an entire night with Diana in my arms is far too tempting to resist.

CHAPTER SEVENTEEN

DIANA

Voicemail message one: Hello, Amanda, my dearest, oldest friend.

I hope everything is okay with you and yours.

If you were a normal person, I would be very worried that you haven't responded to my voice messages from over a week ago, but thankfully I understand that you are not a normal person. I realize that you're as stubborn as a dog sniffing a fence post covered in other dogs' urine, determined to pinpoint exactly who sprayed the post when and whether they were in heat at the time, and that you are also probably suffering from telephonophobia.

Which is a real thing, in case you didn't know.

I've been doing some research on phobias. They're a lot more widespread than you might think.

Voicemail cut off, message sent...

Voicemail message two: So, you see, I understand that you

likely suffer from this phobia and are also maybe trying to teach me to text instead of call by stubbornly refusing to engage with me until I contact you via your approved method of communication. But what you don't understand, my dearest, sweetest friend, is that I cannot text you right now because I am terrified to put the things I'm thinking about saying into writing.

I'm not even sure I can speak them, let alone write them down where I will be forced to look at them in word form and potentially come across them later when I'm scrolling through our text messages trying to find your address because I can never remember where you live when I'm trying to send you weird things I think—

Voicemail cut off, message sent...

Voicemail message three: Remember that time I sent you the merman ornaments with the glittery tails for your Christmas tree? The cowboy merman and the fireman merman and the random, scary-fabulous merman holding a skull and carrying a sparkly pink purse?

Remember how happy you were when you unwrapped them, and how they are now your very favorite ornaments and you save them to put on the tree last every year? Not to brag, but that's something only a good friend who understands your weirdness like no one else does would do, Amanda.

You know another thing a good friend would do?

Pick up the phone before—

Voicemail cut off, message sent...

Voicemail message four: Just please call me back, okay? I promise I'll keep it short and not waste any of your valuable time. Please? Please, please, please?

Or at least text that you're okay? If I don't hear back from you in a day or two, I'm going to call your mom, and you know that never ends well.

For you.

I, on the other hand, will be sent homemade monkey bread as a reward for being concerned about my oldest friend and listening to your mother talk about bird watching and debate for an hour about which brand of hiking boots she should buy. Which I am happy to do because I haven't started my new job yet and my own mother also hates to talk on the phone.

Love you. Call me?

From the texts of Amanda Esposito
and Diana Daniels

Amanda: DO NOT CALL MY MOTHER!
DON'T EVEN THINK ABOUT IT!

Diana: Well, hello to you, too. How's life down there in Eugene where you are apparently so busy you can't spare five seconds to call your very best friend?

Amanda: I worked two doubles last week, Dee. And my allergies have been acting up. By the time I had a spare second to call you, I barely had a voice left, and right now I sound like a goblin that lives under a damp, drafty, pollen-coated bridge. It hurts to talk, but I'm happy to text you through whatever crisis has you so upset.

DIANA: I can't text it. I seriously can't.
The thought of writing it down makes me sick to my stomach.
I know I left silly messages, but I don't feel silly.
I feel scared…

AMANDA: What are you scared of, pumpkin?
Is someone being mean to you?

DIANA: No. The opposite.
Someone is being very nice and good to me.
Someone with a penis…

AMANDA: Oh boy…

DIANA: Exactly.

AMANDA: Well, we figured this would happen sooner or later, right?

DIANA: No, we didn't. I swore off men, Mandy.

And I meant it!

I still mean it!

I don't want to have warm, fuzzy, more-than-friends feelings for anyone with a penis ever again. I hate myself for letting this happen!

I'm such a pathetic weakling loser.

AMANDA: You are not any of those things.

You're a wonderful person with a good heart who needs and deserves to be loved. It isn't your fault you've dated the worst men ever. I met most of them, you'll remember, and they truly did seem like lovely, interesting, cute-as-a-button people until they turned out to be assholes who cheated and lied and ruined your credit.

You've just gotten unlucky, girlfriend.

Maybe you were born under a bad star or something.

DIANA: Maybe. Or maybe there's something deeply wrong with me.

Maybe I have a personality flaw you can't see because we grew up together and you're blind to it. The way people with too many cats in their house become blind to the terrible smell of too many cats.

AMANDA: I have very good eyes and, when I'm not suffering from allergies, a keen nose, as well. I am not blind to your personality flaws. I see them quite clearly.

DIANA: Thanks?

I guess?

Amanda: You are impulsive and opinionated, and you like to have your way more than most people I know, but none of those qualities interfere with your lovableness. You're also funny and sweet and entertaining and loyal and a sexy little minx any guy would be lucky to have on his arm.

And maybe you've finally met a guy who's smart enough to see all those things.

I mean, there has to be a break in the bad luck sooner or later, right?

Even Seattle has a sunny day now and then.

Diana: I had a break in the bad luck once.

And I screwed it up.

Which reminds me, I ran into The One I Screwed It Up With, the other day.

Amanda: OMG NO! You didn't?! When? Where?

Diana: On the street, right after my job interview.

He and his fiancée were coming out of a fancy plate shop a few doors down. I mean, I knew he lived in Portland, but what are the freaking odds?

Amanda: Ugh. I'm so sorry.

But at least you looked adorable, right?

Since you'd just come from an interview?

So it could have been worse?

DIANA: It definitely could have been worse.

And my new friend showed up a minute later and kissed me hello like he was dying to get me home and jump my bones. So that was nice, too.

AMANDA: Oh, that's very nice! I like new guy already.

When do I get to meet him?

DIANA: Never!

Probably never…

You're supposed to be telling me to slow down and take it easy and remember how messing with men has made me miserable for a decade, not telling me to jump back into the plague pit and roll around until I'm coughing up blood and have oozing boils all over my body.

AMANDA: You have a knack for repulsive metaphors.

DIANA: Thank you. Plague is still a thing you can catch, by the way. In case you were wondering. It's carried by rodents in rural areas and is still nearly one hundred percent fatal if not immediately treated by antibiotics.

AMANDA: Another reason never to engage with nature.

DIANA: No, just a reason to go to the doctor if you feel sick instead of thinking you can cure everything with Echinacea and Vitamin C.

AMANDA: Preaching to the choir, babe. We almost lost a woman the other day because she'd waited too long to come in for a thyroid problem.

DIANA: I like that you're smart and agree with me about most things.

AMANDA: I like this, too. But as far as love is concerned…
Well, Sam was a wonderful guy. No arguments there.
But he's not the only wonderful guy in the world.
Maybe losing him is what you needed to teach you to hold on tight the next time someone perfect for you comes along. And maybe it's time to think about holding on to someone again.

DIANA: God…
I seriously almost threw up, Mandy.
Thinking about holding on tight makes me physically ill with terror.

AMANDA: Then you should talk to someone other than me, sweet pea.
I get through life with telephonophobia okay now that most decent human beings understand that texting is better than interrupting someone's perfectly calm existence with a bunch of noisy, stressful ringing. But love-a-phobia is a different animal.
It's like oxygen-a-phobia.

Or cheese-a-phobia.

DIANA: Cake-o-phobia.

AMANDA: Wine-o-phobia.

DIANA: Hike-o-phobia.

AMANDA: You lost me there. Why walk in a circle in the middle of a bunch of trees, where you could be eaten by bears or contract the plague, when you could be walking around an art gallery or museum? Or just window shopping?

DIANA: But what if it's not love-a-phobia, Mandy?
What if I'm a love-a-holic? And instead of giving this thing with New Penis a shot, I should be taking it one day at a time, talking to an anti-love sponsor and counting how many days I've been sober?

AMANDA: Do you seriously think that's true?

DIANA: I don't know! But this feels like falling off the wagon.
I mean, I've never been on the wagon, but this about-to-lose-control-in-the-bad-way feeling is probably what it feels like, right?

Amanda: I hear you.
Hmmmm...
Okay, so how about this...
Ask yourself—and answer honestly—
Are you falling in love with love? Or are you loving being with this particular guy and his particular penis?

Diana: I AM NOT IN LOVE WITH ANYONE OR ANYTHING!
I SAID I WAS TEMPTED TO HAVE FEELINGS NOT THAT I ALREADY HAVE THEM! YOU'RE TAKING THIS WAY TOO FAR WAY TOO FAST! JESUS CONSTIPATED CHRIST, AMANDA, SLOW YOUR DAMN ROLL!

Amanda: STOP ALL CAPS YELLING AT ME, OR I WILL NEVER PICK UP THE PHONE WHEN YOU CALL EVER AGAIN! YOU'RE MAKING MY EYES HURT!

Diana: FINE! IT'S NOT LIKE YOU'RE GOING TO PICK UP ANYWAY!

Amanda: Let's have a time out and text more later.

Diana; No! We don't need a time out! Don't leave me! I'm sorry...
The L-word made my mouth fill with terrible-tasting spit.
Stress spit.
It's awful.

And it made me shouty.
Are you still there?

AMANDA: I'm still here.
So which is it?
The general feeling…
Or the particular person?

DIANA: I…
I don't know…
I was feeling pretty low and lonely when I met this guy…
And it's nice not to feel low or lonely anymore.
Maybe it's the absence of loneliness that's got me feeling soft and squishy, and not this person at all?

AMANDA: So he has no adorable qualities?

DIANA: Well, of course he has adorable qualities.
He's sweet and generous and funny and supportive. And a fucking pleasure to look at in clothing and without clothing and in all the stages in between.
And he called the women who were mean to me at my first interview bitches and took my side when his pig bit me and pulled some strings with a friend to help me land my new job, so…

AMANDA: And the sex isn't gross?

DIANA: *eggplant emoji* *sparkling star emoji* *unicorn emoji* *cartwheel emoji*

AMANDA: Well, that looks promising!

DIANA: He's a dick sorcerer.
 A sorcerer of dick.

AMANDA: And he's not homeless or jobless or secretly a serial killer?

DIANA: As one of the recently underemployed, I take offense to the insinuation that jobless people are unlovable. But no, he's not any of those things. Though he is of above average intelligence, so if he were a secret serial killer, he would probably be clever enough to make sure I didn't find out about it.

AMANDA: So does that make it okay? If he's a serial killer, but you don't know?

DIANA: Well, of course not, but I can't know what I don't know. You know?

AMANDA: And you've just solved your own problem.

DIANA: What? How?

AMANDA: You can't know the unknown. Which means you can't know if New Guy is a keeper unless you give him a chance.

DIANA: Even though every other guy I've given a chance has been awful except one?

AMANDA: He's not every other guy.
He's New Guy.
He's the funny, clever, supportive Dick Sorcerer.

DIANA: God…

AMANDA: No, I'm Amanda.
But I will accept tithing in the form of sex toys. I think it's time to buy a vibrator, but I'm too embarrassed to even order it online. The government is spying on our search histories, you know, and I don't want creepy FBI agents knowing what I'm doing with my vagina in my spare time.
So will you send me one?
One that's good at making a girl not miss her ex?

DIANA: Yes, I will. Because I love you, and I'm so glad you're not getting back together with Wonderdick.

AMANDA: Thanks. I love you, and I'm glad you're going to give love another shot. I firmly believe that someday you're going to make a tolerant man who can stomach talking on the phone very happy.

DIANA: You will talk to me the next time I call.
Third time's a charm...

AMANDA: Keep dreaming, crazy.
And good luck.
I'm rooting for you.

CHAPTER EIGHTEEN

Phone call transcript from Diana Daniels
and Tanner Nowicki

DIANA: Hey...
   You picked up...

TANNER: That's usually what people do when they receive a phone call.

DIANA: Not everyone.
   Some people let it go to voicemail.
   Or refuse the call and answer with a text.

TANNER: I'm not going to refuse a call from you if I can help it.

DIANA: *unintelligible snuffling sound*

TANNER: Diana? You still there?

DIANA: I am…
Thanks for picking up.

TANNER: You're welcome.
What's up? You okay? Is Wanda behaving herself?

DIANA: Yeah. Thanks. I'm good. And Wanda's good.
Are we still on for the Good Timber grand opening party when you get back from Seattle?

TANNER: It's the only thing on my list I'm sure I'm not going to forget.

DIANA: Sweet.

TANNER: Yeah… Are you sure you're okay?

DIANA: Yeah, I'm good.
Really good. I just miss you, I guess.

TANNER: I miss you, too. I can't wait to be kissing distance from your lips again.

DIANA: I'm pretty excited about that, too.

TANNER: Good. Counting the hours, Beach Pixie.

DIANA: Sweet dreams, Muscle Boy.

CHAPTER NINETEEN

TANNER

The Pacific Northwest Super Skills charity event—a daylong battle for bragging rights between the Portland Badgers and the Seattle Storm—is our only official NHL-sanctioned event before the pre-season starts in September. Last year, it was so early in July that I hadn't made the move from the minors to Portland yet, and didn't get a chance to skate.

Which means, for the purposes of today's festivities, I'm still considered a rookie and will be hitting the ice with the rest of the under twenty-fives in the penultimate scrimmage of the game.

It's also my first competitive event since I fell for my captain's little sister and started spending several of the hours I used to spend watching game tape hanging by the pool with Diana, cooking elaborate dinners with Diana, or fantasizing about Diana and wishing she were home with me instead of wherever she's gotten off to while I was at the gym.

I asked her to come to Seattle with me, but we couldn't find anyone to take care of Wanda on such short notice—at least not anyone we could trust her not to attack when their back was turned—so Diana stayed home.

I miss her like oxygen, but it's probably for the best. I'm hoping to steal a few minutes to talk to Brendan about the recent developments in mine and Diana's relationship, and on the off chance Brendan decides to kick my ass, that's something best done without Dee anywhere nearby.

I arrive at the arena around nine a.m. to discover the Seattle locker room is as stinky as I remember, and that the equipment manager has put me in the stall right next to Brendan's. It feels like a sign, but I can't decide if it's a good one or a bad one. Either way, I know better than to try to talk to Brendan before we've taken care of business. He's notoriously no-nonsense in his pregame rituals, and he's sitting next to Justin, who is clearly deep into the focus-enhancing meditation he swears turns his game around every time he's on the schneide or just sucking more than he would like.

And I have my own rituals that need tending to.

I pull up my pregame playlist, slipping in my ear buds and letting my agitated morning brain be soothed by the airy notes of the Peruvian pan flute. It doesn't pump me up the way my old, minor-league playlist used to, but I've learned what my mind wants and what it needs are two different things. With the flutes whistling calmly in my ears, I head out to the ice, leaning my hands against the glass. This is usually when I visualize my positioning during different game situations, keeping in mind the Badger system. Today, however, we'll be playing three on three, so I allow my mind to drift from the usual script, imagining various fast-paced scrimmage scenarios.

Even if this is just a charity event, I need it to go well. I need to prove to myself—and my captain—that I can be crazy about his sister and a force to be reckoned with in my game at the same time.

Twenty minutes later, we hit the ice for warm-ups and then settle onto the bench as our heavy shooters get ready for the first event—a hardest shot contest, where pucks will be clocked as they zip into the net to see which players have the gnarliest slap shot. The Storm players are pale, lean men who look mildly Vitamin D deprived from living in a city where it rains one-hundred and fifty-two days a year. But last summer they ran away with the records for fastest shot and shooting accuracy, while Adams scored the only title for our team, coming in first for skate speed.

This year, Coach Swindle isn't fucking around, sending our biggest and bulkiest out for the slap shot contest, with Petrov's Easter-ham-sized biceps being our best chance at a win. I'm as tall as the rest of the guys hitting the ice, but leaner, so I'll be skating in the final event with Adams and Scroll, who are so jack-rabbit fast I've got no chance in hell of getting around them, which is sort of a relief. I can save my big push for the rookie scrimmage, where I'll be playing with a few two-way contract guys who just started with the Badger's minor league farm team.

As we hoped, Petrov brings home the fastest slap shot—clocking in at one hundred and one miles per hour—but Brendan and Justin, two of our most reliable when it comes to accuracy, are shut out by the Storm's snipers. They return to the bench looking pissed and glaring daggers at the nearly seven-foot tall, quietly ruthless Seattle player who bested them.

"Way to blow it out there, Daniels," Justin says, plopping onto the bench and snatching his water bottle from the shelf.

"Fuck you, Justin," Brendan returns. "You couldn't hit the ass end of an elephant if it were holding still today."

"I know." Justin sniffs, swiping his glove across his sweat-damp upper lip. "But you're supposed to be better than I am. You're Yoda to my Skywalker."

"He's old enough to be Yoda," Petrov says, getting a laugh from both of them.

"Fuck you, too, Petrov," Brendan says, still smiling. "You're only a few years younger than I am, asshole."

"Which is why you can't quit," Petrov says. "I'm not ready to be the geezer of this team."

I observe the exchange, but don't join in the way I usually would. I don't want to risk making Brendan crankier than he is already. Hopefully he and the other over-thirties will crush the Storm in the veteran's scrimmage that closes out the event, and he'll be in a good mood for a nice, calm, reasonable chat afterward.

As predicted, in the speed skate I am thoroughly smoked by the smaller, speedier members of my own team, but I come in ahead of all three Storm players, giving my spirits a lift going into the rookie scrimmage. We're playing three on three, so we'll have more room to navigate, and the action will be more free-flowing and fast-paced than a traditional game. Add in the fact that defense is always more lax in these exhibition matches and I'm looking forward to getting flashy with my offense and showing off a few puck-handling tricks I've been working on.

I hit the ice with the two minor-league guys I recognize from our franchise end-of-the-year party, and for the first of our two abbreviated eighteen-minute periods, we proceed to kick Storm rookie ass. We've never played together before, but the chemistry is there from the drop of the puck. The open format gives the minor leaguers the chance to shine, allowing them to showcase speed and talent that leaves no doubt I'll be seeing them around the Badger locker room before too long. And they're not selfish with the puck, either. They set me up with several tic-tac-toe plays, and I send the puck sailing into the open net, earning two of our four goals and ensuring our second period is pure playtime.

It is a fact universally acknowledged that there are certain moves best avoided during a regular season game if you prefer your head to remain attached to the rest of your body. But in a three-on-three scrimmage when you're already up four goals? Well, then, anything goes.

I start off the second period by intercepting a pass and scooping it up, carrying it on the blade of my stick and shooting it into the net lacrosse style, inches in front of the Storm rookie chasing me down the ice. My linemates and I continue our scoring onslaught by racking up two more goals, all while grinning like kids kicking ass in a pond hockey massacre after school.

I can't remember the last time I've had so much fun, and by the time I put an end to the scoring by faking out the goalie, aborting my forehand shot to seal the deal by tapping the biscuit between my legs into the net, I'm flying higher than I have in a long while.

Taking the game seriously is important for my future and my career, but I wouldn't have a career without my love of being on the ice.

Back on the bench, things are quieter than I expect them to be, until Petrov calls out, "Where you been hiding the mad skills, rookie," and laughter erupts from the rest of the team.

"Fancy footwork, man," Adams says as I sit down beside him. "You were on fire out there."

"I'm going to talk to Coach about letting you off the leash more, Nowicki." Brendan gives me an encouraging slap on the back. "You've got improv skills we should be taking advantage of. You keep playing like that, and you'll be a top-six forward before you know it."

And that right here—praise from the captain who had to pull me aside several times last season for impromptu therapy sessions when my game started to suffer—is one of the highlights of my year. The only thing that could get me any higher is hearing Brendan say that he trusts me to be the kind of boyfriend his sister deserves.

The veteran game is tighter, but Brendan scores twice, Petrov continues his lucky streak with two goals, and we take home the vet scrimmage win by a comfortable two-point margin.

We head down the tunnel feeling no pain, and the locker room is filled with the familiar "we crushed it" vibe that always follows a win. Laughter and conversation are louder than usual, and a plan to meet up for beers after we touch down in Portland triggers a debate about which microbrewery has the best happy hour.

I couldn't ask for better timing to declare my completely honorable intentions toward Brendan's sister. Naively, I think the festive atmosphere will make this easier.

I am, however, very, very wrong.

"What the fuck did you just say to me?" Brendan asks in a chillingly quiet voice after a silence that has already stretched on for way too long.

I swallow hard. "I'm going to ask Diana is she wants to start dating. Seriously. Exclusively."

Justin, who has clearly overheard what was supposed to be a private conversation, lets out a long, low whistle. "Oh, you stupid, stupid rookie."

"I know dating a teammate's family is frowned on," I hurry to add. "But I care about Diana and she—"

"Caring about her is fine," Brendan cuts in, dropping his bag with a heavy *thunk* that echoes in the increasingly quiet locker room. "Fucking my little sister, who I trusted with you because I was certain you had the good judgment to keep your dick in your pants, is something else. What the hell were you thinking?"

"I was thinking she's a really cool person." I stand my ground as he takes a menacing step forward. "She's funny and smart and interesting, and I don't want to let my shot with her slip through my fingers because of some stupid team rule."

Brendan's lips part, but I push on before he can speak.

"And it is stupid." I lift my chin, meeting his cold gaze without looking away. "A rule against casual shit is fine, sure. But what I feel for Diana isn't casual, and I'm not going anywhere until she tells me to get lost. You can kick my ass if you feel that's necessary, but all I want to do is make her happy. I'm going to be good to her. You can count on that."

Brendan shakes his head, the muscle in his jaw clenching and unclenching until he finally waves a dismissive hand. "Fine. Knock yourself out, Nowicki. But I hope you realize she's a grown woman. She's not some puck bunny who's going to be impressed by the fact that you play pro hockey, and she's already been through hell with boys who didn't know how to act like men. Don't be one of them, or I will make sure the rest of your time on this team is as brief and unpleasant as I can possibly make it."

"I've been a grown man since I was eighteen," I say, unable to keep the anger from my voice. "I also have two sisters of my own, who I love too much to treat other women like shit. You've known me for a year. I would think the fact that I'm not a jackass have been made pretty clear by now."

"What's clear is that you have poor listening skills," Brendan says, reclaiming his bag. "And even worse impulse control."

My lips part to defend myself, but he's already gone, storming out of the locker room with Justin not far behind.

Jus pauses at the door to pin me with a "you really stepped in it this time" look that isn't without a certain degree of pity, then ducks out to follow Brendan, hopefully to put in a good word for me.

Justin and I are closer than we were when I was first drafted onto the team. I helped facilitate his proposal for God's sake. Surely he can do me a solid and tell Brendan he has no reason to believe I'll be anything but a good boyfriend.

I reach for my own bag, only to jump in surprise when I realize Petrov is standing beside me. "Shit," I say, breath rushing out. "How are you so big and so quiet at the same time?"

"Practice." He studies me beneath his furrowed brow. "Some things you can only learn from experience, but I'm willing to share mine if you're willing to listen. I believe I've proven I was spot-on about the thin line between hate and fucking."

I nod slowly. "Fine. What do you think I should do?"

"I think you should call it off with Diana, apologize to your captain, and get your focus back where it belongs—on your team. You treat it right, and this team will be your family for a good, long while. A hot summer with a firecracker might be fun, but it isn't worth putting your future at risk."

"She isn't just a firecracker." I keep my voice soft so the nosy bastards on their way to the showers can't eavesdrop. "I've never felt this way about someone before. Ever. And yes, I get it, this team can feel like a family. But I would like a real family someday. Wife, kids, the whole package."

Petrov's thick brows lift. "How long have you known Dee? A week?"

"Over three weeks."

He makes a disgusted sound. "Love at first sight isn't a real thing, kid. Trust me."

"It wasn't at first sight," I protest. "We didn't—"

"You can't fall in real love in a few weeks," he cuts in. "You're letting your dick be your guide, which isn't always a bad thing, but in this case it absolutely is. You're going to wake up out of this fuck-happy fog in a few months and wonder what you were thinking. But by then it will be too late. You'll already be in a shitty place with your captain and your team and have proven that you aren't someone we can trust. And you won't like the way it feels to be outside the trust circle, kid. Believe me."

"I'm not a kid," I say, the fact that those particular words are coming out of my mouth making me feel about twelve fucking years old. "And I know the difference between a hard-on and something more."

Petrov's dark eyes grow even darker. "I thought I did, too. And then she stole my grandmother's car and my credit cards, took off to Vegas, and never came back."

I wince. "Ouch."

"And up until the day she left, I thought it was real," he says, opening up more than he ever has with me. "And no, not every woman is after your money or your fame or your grandmother's car, but there are enough of them out there that you need to start being really fucking careful. Take things slow and then take them even slower. The right woman will wait, while the wrong ones move on to an easier mark."

I shake my head. "Diana isn't like that. I'm the one who wants more. I'm pretty sure she would be fine with keeping things casual."

"Diana is good people," he says. "But she never should have been on the menu. For her sake, as well as yours. Think of how shitty she'll feel if she realizes she's the reason Brendan isn't willing to be an advocate for you anymore? Because you realize there's no way he's having that talk with

Coach now, right? That ship has been shot full of canon balls and is sinking fast."

I let out a long sigh. "I know, but…" I trail off, shaking my head as I shrug my bag over my shoulder. "But I don't care. She's worth it."

Petrov grunts. "Well, good luck, then. I hope I'm wrong, I really do."

My lips curve in a bitter grin. "But you think there's a better chance of pigs flying out of my butt."

"Or of you letting me butcher that pet of yours," he agrees, clapping me on the shoulder. "But at least love seems to agree with your game."

It agrees with more than my game. It agrees with every part of me—body and soul—and sooner or later Brendan is going to realize that Diana and I are the reason the family rule shouldn't exist. We're good together and getting better every day. I'm certain of that. As certain as I am that when I meet Diana at the party tonight, she'll greet me with silly stories about what she and Wanda did while I was away, and an extra sunny smile just for me.

Yes, I'm really *that* naïve. God help me.

CHAPTER TWENTY

DIANA

Late Wednesday afternoon, I dress in a sparkly blue dress and head for the door, only to change my mind and run back upstairs to change into a light brown sundress with woodland creatures embroidered on the bodice and the hem. I'm afraid the blue will be too sparkly, and I figure I can't go wrong with a woodland creature theme, considering the venue.

When I arrive at Good Timber's St. Johns location twenty minutes later, I'm relieved to learn my gut hasn't led me astray. The assembled company—my soon-to-be coworkers, their spouses, and various friends of the brewery—are a handsome crew, but not an overly dressy one. There's an easy, breezy vibe to the party, and I'm able to jump away from a leaking keg tap a lot faster in my white sandals than I could have in gold pumps.

Once I've secured a pint of Cranberry Cougar, I track Jax down at the bocce ball court in the back patio area and thank him for the invite.

"Of course. So glad you could make it." His brown eyes flick up and down my frame in a way that is appreciative without being skeezy. Truly an art most men have yet to master, proving my new boss is a keeper. "Love your dress. You're already earning us trendy cred just by showing up."

"Well, thank you," I say, deciding it's too early to confess that I'm one of the least on-trend people I know. Hopefully I'll have a chance to impress him with my work before he realizes that my fashion sense is only on-point about a third of the time.

Jax smiles "I'm glad you invited Tanner, by the way. We haven't had a chance to have a beer and catch up in a while."

"I'll be sure to bring him by for a chat once he gets here," I promise, easing away as two serious-looking men in suits sidle up to Jax, looking needy. "Catch you later."

"Later." Jax lifts a hand before turning to give the suits his attention.

I wander through groups of people engaged in conversation, card games, or prolonged study of the art that's been hung on the back wall of the main dining room since the last time I was here. I marvel again how a party is something different to every person who attends. Some of these people are having a laugh-out-loud silly time with close friends, some are engaged in urgent, hushed discussions about business or personal matters, and some, like me, are circling the perimeter, looking for people who seem like they might be amenable to welcoming a newbie into their midst.

Thankfully, despite my years of solitude in the woods, I seem to remember how this "being social" thing works. I spot a group of mixed company—two friendly-looking girls and three guys who are playing darts with some very cool looking feathered arrows—and fold myself into their conversation with minimal fuss. They prove to be every bit as friendly as I'd hoped they would, as well as understanding about my poor aim.

After thirty minutes and another beer, I drift away from

my new friends to visit the ladies, check the time—still over an hour until Tanner gets here, dammit—and apply a fresh coat of lip gloss. I'm debating whether to rejoin my pals or to strike out in search of more friendly faces, when I emerge from the ladies room and run smack into the last person I expect to see.

"Sam!" His name emerges with a breathy laugh as I step back, pulling my hands away from his chest with an "I've been burned" swiftness. I haven't touched him in so long, and it feels immediately, intensely wrong.

We aren't people who touch. Not anymore, not ever again.

"What are you doing here?" I ask, blinking fast.

His lips tremble into an uncertain smile, but instead of saying he's here to cover the opening for one of the magazines he writes for, as I'm anticipating, he opens his mouth and crazy things come out. "I'm here to see you, actually."

I turn my head sharply to one side and blink again. "I'm sorry?"

He laughs. "No, I'm sorry. That came out wrong. I'm part of the Wood Timber tasting club. They send out an email blast every week, keeping members up to date on the brewery news. Yesterday they sent out a blast about the opening, with a list of the staff who will be working at the new location. I saw your name in the PR position and I just..." He shakes his head. "It felt like a sign, running into you twice in one week after so long wondering where you were and how you were doing."

"That is kind of a crazy coincidence." I step back, moving out of the way of two women weaving their way toward the bathroom.

His brow furrows as he jabs a thumb over his shoulder. "Can we talk, do you think? Catch up somewhere private?"

I nod a little too fast, stretching a hand toward the patio and the business offices beyond. "Sure. We could head to the staff break room if you want. I would take you to my office, but I have no idea where it is yet. I don't officially start until next week."

"Sounds good," he says, following me down the hall. "So what made you decide to make the move to Portland? I thought we'd never get you out of the woods."

"I still love the woods, but I got tired of being the poorest person I knew. I don't mind suffering for my art, but it was time to see if I could find a way to improve my bottom line. And I have family here, of course."

"I remember. How is your brother?"

"Good!" I force a cheery smile. "He's engaged, too."

"Good for him," Sam says, before smoothly turning the conversation back to safer waters. "And good for you. Good Timber's a great company."

We talk shop—the usual grumblings about working in a creative profession in the digital age—as we leave the party and head down the cobblestone path to a smaller courtyard surrounded by the Good Timber offices. I lead the way to the break room; it's a cozy space with a small bar, complete with two beers on tap, bistro tables and stools, and a kitchenette against the far wall, and as we go in, I deliberately leave the door open behind us.

I don't know why, but I feel weird about being alone in an enclosed space with Sam. Obviously, we're just friends now —or on our way to being friends, I guess, if he's gone to all the trouble to track me down for a chat—but the memory of intimacies lurk beneath the surface, and sometimes open doors are as good at marking boundaries as closed ones. I can't think about the fact that I used to make love to this man —sweet, sexy, no-holding-back love—or I'll do something mortifying like blush bright red or cry. The way I cried the day Sam told me we were never going to have a second chance because he'd fallen in love with someone else while we were taking a break for me to figure my shit out.

"So what's up?" I circle the bar. "Would you like a beer? Looks like we've got Hipster Honey and a pale ale on draft."

"No, thanks." Sam leans against the entrance to the bar, blocking my path out, unknowingly feeding my ex-encounter anxiety. "I don't want to keep you from the party for too long. I just thought…" He trails off, studying his hand as his fingers spread wide on the polished wood. "This is a beautiful piece."

"It is," I agree, beginning to think I'm not the only one who's feeling awkward. A long moment passes in silence before I add in a softer voice, "This doesn't have to be weird, Sam. I know I was a mess when we broke up for good, but I'm okay now. And I'm happy for you. It seems like Madeline is a beautiful person, inside and out." I smile, a little surprised to find I mean it.

I *am* happy for him, something that wouldn't have been possible before Tanner.

Damn. *Tanner.*

Just thinking about him makes me feel like I've swallowed sunshine. I've got it bad. Worse than I had it for Sam a few weeks into our relationship, that's for damned sure, and look how far down the love road we went together.

I'm so distracted by this realization—and the simultaneously terrifying and exciting suspicion that Tanner might be that even more perfect-for me-than-Sam guy I never dreamed I'd find—that I don't realize Sam is within touching distance until his hand settles on mine, pinning me between his warm skin and the cool wood of the bar.

I look up to find him staring at me with an intensity that

throws me off center. "What's wrong?" I ask, brow furrowing.

"Madeline is wonderful," he says. "But she's not you."

I gape at him, eyes wide, so shocked that all I can do is open and close my mouth like a startled goldfish as Sam leans closer.

CHAPTER TWENTY-ONE

DIANA

"I know this is crazy, but seeing you the other day brought back so many memories. Of you and me and how good it was. It never felt like work with you. It was easy, as natural as breathing." Sam smiles wistfully, clearly having no clue this conversation is giving me a golf-ball sized lump in my throat. "And the way we would laugh..." He chuckles fondly. "Jesus, no one's ever made me laugh the way you do."

"And no one's ever made me cry the way you did," I say, voice hoarse. I pull my hand from beneath his, crossing my arms. "I know it was my fault for calling a time-out in the first place, but damn it, Sam. When you said we were never getting another chance because you'd met someone else..." I swallow hard, fighting the emotion churning in my chest. "I thought I was going to die. I wanted to for a while. I couldn't imagine how I would ever feel okay again."

He reaches up, cupping my face in one big hand. "I'm sorry."

My breath rushes out. "You don't have to be sorry. Like I

said, I know it was my fault, too. I'm the one who needed a break."

"Because you'd just come out of a shitty relationship," he says, thumb brushing back and forth across my cheek, making me feel sick with a mixture of regret, longing, and confusion.

What is even happening here?

"What do you want, Sam?" I take another step away. My final step, I realize as my ass hits the mini fridge. "Why are you saying these things now? After two years without so much as an email?"

"Because I've spent the past month registering for gifts for a wedding I'm not sure I want to go through with anymore," he says, a haunted look creeping into his blue eyes. "I thought Madeline was the right choice. She's solid and steady and always perfectly put together, and she made me feel like a fucking grown-up for the first time in my life. And then I saw you again, with your hair all crazy and your every thought flashing across your face, and I just..." He shifts closer, brow furrowing miserably. "I remembered how good it was to be with someone who wasn't afraid to be different. To be completely herself, no matter what."

"Who the hell else am I supposed to be?"

"Someone other people find easier to digest," he says. "You're supposed to wad yourself into a box the way the rest of us do, but you don't. It's one of the things I love most about you."

I suck in a deeper breath, trying to stop the room from spinning. "Shit, Sam, I don't—"

"I need to be sure, Diana," he cuts in, taking my cold hand. "Don't you want to be sure we haven't made a huge mistake hooking up with other people?"

"You're not hooking up, you're getting married," I protest.

"And Tanner and I just started getting sort of serious. I could never—"

"Then it's even easier for you," Sam says, a manic light in his eyes. "If it's that new, you can just tell him you want to keep seeing other people for a while. And then you and I will have time to get to know each other again before we decide who we want to be with long term."

I gulp in air. "This is crazy, Sam. What about Madeline? No way is she going to go from registering for wedding gifts to being okay with you dating your ex for a few months. And I don't—"

"That's why I can't tell her." He gives my hand a firm squeeze. "We would have to keep it a secret from Maddie until we know for sure that you and I want to get back together."

My head rears back, knocking into the wall behind me.

"Ouch. Are you okay?" Sam asks.

"No." I pull my hand from his as my heart begins to drag in my chest and a wave a dread rises inside me. "No, I'm not okay. I can't…"

"I know it isn't ideal," Sam says. "But I think it's important that we both keep our other options open. That way we know we're choosing each other because it's the right choice, not because it's the *only* choice."

I shake my head, blinking fast. "I can't believe this is happening."

He braces his hands on either side of my face. "I know. It's a big step, but it feels right, doesn't it?"

An unexpected laugh bursts from my tight throat. "No, Sam. It doesn't feel right! What is wrong with you? What in the course of our relationship ever made you think I would be okay with fucking around behind another woman's back? Any woman, but especially one as completely sweet and decent as Madeline?"

"It wouldn't be like that," he says, having the gall to sound wounded.

"It would be exactly like that." I duck under his arm and hurry out from behind the bar, no longer able to tolerate being trapped so close to him. "And I can't, Sam. I just can't with you right now."

"Then take some time." He follows me as I rush for the door. "Think on it and let me know when you—"

"I don't need time." I spin back, pointing a shaking finger at his chest, silently warning him to keep his distance. "I don't need a God damned second. I already know that you and this plan both make me sick. I can't believe I thought you were the one good man I'd ever dated."

He scowls, shaking his head like I'm the one who's crossed the line. "You didn't used to be like this, Diana. You used to understand that the world wasn't black and white. You used to enjoy coloring outside the lines."

I huff softly, fighting the tears pressing at the backs of my eyes. "The fact that you can't see the difference between creativity and lying, deception, and infidelity is telling, Sam."

"And dating a jock with the IQ of a wet sponge clearly hasn't been good for you," he counters, startling me with that new bitter streak of his again.

"I don't know if you've changed," I say softly, "or if I was just too young and stupid and in love to see you clearly before, but this is never going to happen. I don't want to see you, Sam. Not ever again."

Ignoring his call for me to wait, I turn and run through the open door, tears slipping down my cheeks and breath burning in my chest. I don't know why I'm crying at first, only that it feels like the entire world is crumbling around me and there's no safe place to hide.

But hide I eventually do, in the last stall of the women's bathroom, where I fall apart for a good twenty minutes, muffling my sobs in the crook of my arm until I finally realize why I'm so upset, and then my tears shut off like someone spun a spigot inside my head.

Just like that, in a burst of fully realized, Technicolor, 3D horror, I understand that Sam turning out to be a creep doesn't simply mean that I was taken in by a scam artist who somehow convinced me he was the sweetest man I'd ever met. No, it means something much worse. It means that I have never picked a decent man.

I have *never* had a healthy relationship. I have *never* been loved by someone who cared as much for me as he did for himself, let alone who cared for me *more*. Who cared the way people are supposed to care when they fall in love.

I am a complete loser failure, which can only mean one thing—

"Tanner isn't real." It hurts like a knife stabbed into my sternum, sending bone slivers into my heart, but it's true. It has to be true. Sure, my stupid brain thinks he might be "the One," but my stupid brain is stupid.

So stupid. So fucking stupid and blind and ridiculous.

I wasted a significant portion of my life mourning a man who's ready to cheat on his new wife before they even get to the altar. I flirted with dark, self-destructive thoughts because of him. I swore off love and passion because I'd convinced myself Sam had been my one shot and I fucked it up.

Though, honestly, that last part was probably the only smart thing I've ever done as far as my love life is concerned. I clearly have no business getting involved with anyone. Ever. Even Seattle has a sunny day now and then, but I'm zero for ten years and over a dozen men, without a single one of my Prince Charmings turning out to be anything but a frog or a fraud.

I have to end this thing with Tanner now. Before it's too

late. Before I have to see a person I truly believe is a wonderful, sexy, sweet one-in-a-million man turn out to be the biggest disappointment of all.

Whipping out my phone, I write Tanner a long, slightly hysterical but honest and apologetic email wishing him a beautiful future without me in it. I read it over twice, overcome by this miserable but necessary and urgent feeling like my body is on the verge of purging something poisonous.

This hope is poisonous. Or the loss of it will be.

I can't do this again. I can't get sucked into dreaming and wishing, only to have it turn to ash when the man I've fallen in love with pulls his mask away, revealing the rotten reality beneath.

I'm done with love, this addiction that's done nothing but push me off a series of ever higher and more dangerous ledges. I need to stick to my guns and my promises and be done with romance once and for all.

Sucking in a bracing breath, I hit send on the email and make a run for it, slipping out of the party before any of my new coworkers can see my splotchy face or haunted, sad, former love-a-holic eyes.

CHAPTER TWENTY-TWO

TANNER

I've only been at the party a few minutes—long enough to grab a beer and spot Jax deep in conversation with a pretty brunette in the back courtyard—when a text from Diana comes through.

Check your email. I'm so sorry. I hope someday you can forgive me.

Immediately, my stomach is full of writhing snakes and my beer turns to vinegar in my mouth. *Fuck.* I have no idea what this is about, but it's clearly not good. Not fucking good at all.

Setting my pint glass down on the bar, I step outside, circling to the windowless portion of the brick building, not wanting an audience for this. If Diana's email is as bad as I'm anticipating, I'm going to be lucky to avoid slamming a fist into a wall, and that's not the image I like to project in public.

I find the email in question immediately, and from the first line, it's clear the situation is worse than I thought.

To: Nowicki3

From: DeedleDee
Subject: I can't, I'm so sorry…
Dear Tanner,

This isn't an easy email to write, but I truly feel I have no other choice.

Something happened tonight that confirmed my suspicion that I'm either the worst judge of character in the entire world or was born with bad love luck coded into my DNA. There should have been at least one exception to the rule, one man who slipped through my fingers because of mistakes I made instead of his faulty moral compass.

But now I know that's not true. My entire romantic history is one long loser parade, from the first to the last and every jerk in between.

Of course, I want to believe you're different, I really do. In fact, at this moment, I think you're the most amazing guy I've ever been with. You're kind, generous, thoughtful, and fun. You're a dirty dream come to life in the sack, and you make me laugh like no one has in a long time.

But I thought good things about the other men I dated, too. In the beginning, it's so easy to get swept away in a new romance and believe this time things will be different.

And maybe they would have been with us, but I can't take that chance right now. I know I play it tough, but I'm not tough. I'm beaten down and battle-scarred and terrified of what would happen if I had to rumble down the shitty road to Splitsville with you. I know it would be the ugliest, saddest, most painful road I've seen yet, and I'm not sure I have the strength to survive it.

I'm a coward, Tanner. And you deserve better.

If you're the man I think you are, you deserve a sexy, sweet, fearless goddess who will match you and challenge you and love you hard and fierce, with no holding back.

Sadly, I'm not that girl. I was telling the truth that first night on the beach. I can't be the kind of person you need, Muscle Boy, no matter how much I might want to be.

So do yourself a favor and don't waste any regret on me. Just keep being the lovely person you are, and I know you'll find someone wonderful, who will make you happier than I ever could. I wish you so many good things, and I hope maybe someday, after the summer love burn has peeled and faded away, we can be friends. Maybe even good friends.

You are special to me. I hope you know that.

Take care of yourself and that crazy pig. I'll be spending the night at my brother's house and will come by while you're at practice tomorrow to get my things and leave your room ready to be rented to someone more suitable.

Best wishes and sincere regrets,

Diana

The second I'm done reading, I shut the browser and call Diana's cell, but I'm sent immediately to voicemail.

"I got the email, but this isn't done," I say, voice thick with emotion. "We need to talk. Call me back as soon as you get this."

I pace the sidewalk for a few minutes, waiting for a call I know isn't going to come, and then whip my phone from my pocket and type out a quick text: *I'm coming to your brother's house and we're going to talk. This doesn't end with an email, Diana. I'm in too deep for that, and so are you.*

She is. She's falling for me as hard and fast as I'm falling for her. I understand being scared, and I'm willing to give her as much time and space as she needs to realize I'm different than the losers she dated before. I'll back off and take baby steps toward her heart if that's what it takes, but I'm not going to give up on her.

If I give up, the dicks of the world win. And fuck if I'm going to let that happen. At least, not without a fight.

I don't remember getting in my car or pulling out of the parking lot. My body is on autopilot while my mind composes arguments I pray are compelling enough to keep the door to this relationship from slamming in my face.

Ironically, when I ring the doorbell at Brendan's place twenty minutes later, my captain opens the door, pronounces, "Not now, Nowicki," and promptly shuts it.

In my face.

He didn't slam the damned thing, but that doesn't make much difference. The door is still closed, and Diana is on one side while I'm stuck out here alone on the other.

"At least tell her I'm here," I say, raising my voice to be heard through the solid wood. "I just want to talk to her."

"She knows you're here," Brendan calls back. "If she wanted to talk, she would have answered the door herself."

"Please, Brendan," I say, not too proud to beg if that's what it takes to get to Diana. "I don't know what happened to upset her, but it has nothing to do with me. I'm on the right side of history, here, I promise."

"I believe you, rookie," Brendan says in a gentler tone. "But nothing good is going to come from talking to Diana tonight. I know my sister. When she gets like this, she needs space, a good night's sleep, and time for the panic flames to die down. Pushing now is only going to make things worse."

My breath rushes out as I run a clawed hand through my hair. I can't imagine things getting worse than Diana breaking up with me over email before we've even officially started our relationship, but Brendan clearly has no intention of opening the door. "Can you at least tell her I came by?" I ask. "And that I'll wait as long as I need to wait for her to be ready to hear me out?"

"I will," Brendan says. "And don't worry about any fallout

from the team. Diana made me promise not to give you any shit about this. She seems to think you're one of the good ones."

"Just not good enough," I mumble.

I turn, heading down to the street, but halfway across the wide lawn, I pause to look back, scanning the second-story windows for a sign of Diana. But all the curtains are closed, the house's eyes closed tight, its shuttered features offering no reason to hope.

"I don't care. I'm not giving up." I feel silly talking to myself but bolstered by the promise all the same.

I'm not giving up. I'm going to prove to Diana that I'm not another loser to add to the list of men who have let her down. I'm the one she's been waiting for, the one who won't lie or cheat or steal or cause so much as a hairline fracture in her heart.

I'm here to break the curse and wake the princess with a kiss.

Now to find a way to convince the princess to quit pushing me away so I can prove it.

CHAPTER TWENTY-THREE

DIANA

*H*iding in my brother's guest room, I cry myself into a fitful sleep and dream I'm speeding down a crowded highway...

I'm frantic and afraid, desperate to get away from the people who are chasing me. I can't see them yet, but I know they're gunning down the road behind me in a Hummer with spikes on the wheels and rocket launchers on the roof and that they fully intend to carve me into tiny pieces as soon as they run me off the road.

But of course, the rest of the jerks in front of me are driving like assholes, and one particular beat-up white pickup truck refuses to get out of the left lane and let me pass. He keeps puttering along next to the red car beside him, while I pound on my horn, shout for him to "please get the fuck over!" and wish I had superpowers so I could teleport the truck into the ditch before it's too late.

Finally, after what feels like hours of bad-driver torture, the yahoo finally steers into the right lane, and I put the gas pedal to the floor, speeding around him as my heart hiccups in my chest and my brain threatens to have a relief stroke.

Thank God, I'm finally free!

Free and on the move again, fleeing danger faster with every passing second as the road in front of me opens up, revealing miles of clear, uncluttered highway.

I've just started to believe that escape is certain when a slim blonde sprints out of the tall grass to my left and into the path of oncoming traffic.

I gasp in horror and pull my foot from the gas, but before I can hit the brakes, I slam into the woman. I scream as a sickening thud shakes the car and a subsequent *rumble-tumble* sound rattles over my head as the body rolls across the roof and bounces off the trunk and down to the pavement behind me.

Bile rushes up my throat and tears flood my eyes as I skid to a stop on the side of the road, knowing that this is it—the moment my life changes forever. I will never be the innocent, relatively carefree woman I was before. From now until the day I die, I will be a murderer, a monster who mowed down another human being because I was so busy running I let myself drive way too fast.

If I'd been going the speed limit, I still might have hit her, but I would have had time to pump the brakes, and there would have been at least a chance of survival.

But now...

I fall out of the car and stagger toward the back, bracing myself on the sun-warmed metal. There's no doubt in my mind that the woman I hit is dead. The only question is how bad it's going to be.

Somehow, the highway is now empty in both directions, all the other cars vanished out of respect for this moment, this murder, this loss that could have been avoided if I were a different person.

If I were less afraid. If I were the type to turn and face my demons instead of racing as fast as I can away from them.

I'm so deep in dread that my internal organs feel like they're turning to poisonous slime, and then I see her face. My heart stops, my throat closes, and my eyes go so wide it feels like they're trying to rip holes in my skin.

Because the woman lying dead and broken on the road is me.

I BOLT awake in Brendan's guest room, fist pressed to my chest where my heart is pounding on my sternum like a coked-up wrecking ball.

I pull in deep breaths that shudder out through trembling lips, promising myself it was just a dream. But I can't get the image of my own face, glassy-eyed, battered and bloody, out of my head or the taste of terror out of my mouth.

I reach for my phone, needing to hear someone's voice, even if it's only on an answering machine. I expect to get Amanda's voicemail, but much to my surprise, the woman herself answers.

"Good morning," she says cheerfully. "Were your ears burning?"

"Wh-what?" I stammer, tongue slipping out to dampen my nightmare-dry lips.

"Your future sister-in-law called me this morning," Amanda says. "She said that you were in desperate need of an old friend. Lucky for you, I've got the rest of the week and the weekend off, and I'm only twenty minutes outside of Portland."

I blink against the tears that spring suddenly to my eyes. "You're coming to cheer me up?"

"I'm coming to talk sense into you. Unicorn dicks don't come along every day, sweet cheeks. You need to quit freaking out and get back on that stallion."

"You don't understand." I shake my head as I smash a fist

into one aching temple. "Sam is an asshole, too. There's no hope. I'm hopeless. There was hope, but now there is none. At all. Ever."

"We'll see about that," Amanda says. "Get up and get dressed. I'm taking you to brunch. The cheer-upping and sense-talking will commence as soon as we're fed. I need eggs and coffee to be in top persuasive form."

"I can't. I have to get my things from Tanner's place while he's at practice."

"No, you don't," Laura says from the other side of my closed bedroom door. "I called Tanner and told him you won't be able to come get your things until this weekend. You need to go have girl-bonding time with someone you trust."

I scowl at the door, but after my nightmare, I can't seem to get worked up about little things like being spied on or lovingly bullied. "And to think I thought you were a sweet, classy, shy sort of person when we first met, Laura. Which further proves I'm a poor judge of character."

Laura laughs. "It does not. I'm all those things. Sometimes. And sometimes I'm nosy and feel compelled to stick my oar in when someone I love is making a mistake. I would have given you the 'Running Away is a Bad Idea' lecture myself, but you think I'm too grossly in love to be objective about romance."

"Which is why I'm perfect," Amanda says, clearly able to hear Laura on her end of the phone. "My love life is a disaster, and I'm still coming to tell you not to run. So get dressed and prepare to receive my testimony. Be there soon."

Amanda hangs up, Laura offers to bring me coffee, and I realize how little I have to complain about. I might have gotten the short end of the stick when it comes to men, but the friends in my life are really top notch.

When Amanda arrives, we head directly to *Crepe Amusette*

and snag seats in the garden, where the flowers are still damp with dew and the golden morning sunlight gently infers that anything is possible.

"I've Googled your unicorn man, interrogated your brother, and gotten the inside scoop from Laura, who's worked with Tanner since he joined the team," Amanda says. "All signs point to him being a lovely, genuine person. And there is no reason he should have to pay for Sam being a creep, especially since I never liked Sam in the first place."

My eyebrows shoot up. "What? You said he was great!"

"I said that because *you* thought he was great, and I didn't want to disagree since your relationship with him was halfway functional."

"Great." I slug down my espresso, knowing today will require massive amounts of caffeine to keep me upright. "So you're admitting I am the worst at relationships."

"No, I'm admitting you've had bad luck up to this point. But so what? That's no reason to shut down any possibility for future relationship-based happiness." Amanda crosses her arms with a disgusted expression. "I mean, seriously, Dee. When did you have your ovaries taken out? Because last time I checked, you were one of the strongest, bravest people I knew."

My forehead wrinkles. "I don't know. Maybe they were stolen by an organ harvester while I was sleeping. One morning they just weren't there anymore. One morning I woke up and realized I'm trucking hard toward thirty and I still feel like an imposter pretending to be a grown-up, who is no closer to knowing how to make love work than I was at eighteen."

Amanda's deep brown eyes go soft at the center. "And who ever said we had to have it all figured out by thirty? Growing up takes as long as it takes, and hopefully it never stops. You don't want to be one of those smug, pompous, stick-in-the-mud people who think they've got life all figured out, anyway, do you?"

I shake my head, running a finger through the sugar I spilled on the table. "No, but I don't want to be a train wreck, either. And I don't want another bad ending. Especially not with Tanner. He seems so wonderful. It would kill me if he turned out to be another rat."

"No, it wouldn't," Amanda says firmly. "No one ever died from losing at the game of love."

"What about Romeo and Juliet?"

"Fictional, and they were children. That was teenage obsession, not love," Amanda says. "In real life, it's not breakups that bring us down, it's the stories we tell ourselves while the breakup is happening. Stories about how broken and strange and unlovable we are." She leans in, propping her arms on the table. "But those stories aren't true, Dee. All of us deserve to be loved. Especially lovely little weirdos like you."

My eyes fill with tears, but before I can start sobbing, the waiter brings the food, and Amanda calls a time out to concentrate on fueling the body before we fuel our spirits with a girls' day out like no other.

And it really is like no other. We spend the entire day shopping, eating, and wandering around the city like we used to do when we were in college, but this time we talk like grown-ups. We share things we've never shared and confess things we've never confessed, and Amanda opens up about Wonderdick in a way that makes me wish I'd been even more caustic in my criticism of the creep.

"Can I strangle him for you?" I ask, covering her hand with mine. We're two margaritas into happy hour at Bozo Sombrero, a favorite Mexican restaurant decorated in a delightfully disturbing mixture of clown statues and Mexican folk art. "Seriously. He needs to stop breathing."

Amanda purses her lips and exhales, blowing her thick

bangs out of her eyes. "No, you can't strangle him. He's not worth going to jail for, and he has children to support so..."

I shake my head, still having a hard time wrapping my mind around this "secret family" reveal. "So he's been married this entire time? With two kids? And there was never any clue?"

"Not until the phone call in May," Amanda says with a stiff shrug. "He'd always traveled a lot for work, so I didn't think anything of it until I got a call from his wife. He screwed up and left the wrong cell phone plugged in to charge at his house in Sedona. She found it and called to give me the 411. Apparently, he's done this before with a girl in L.A. But they ended up having a kid before he broke the news that he was married to someone else, so I guess I should consider myself lucky things never went that far."

I squeeze her margarita-chilled fingers. "I'm so sorry, Mandy. He's the worst. He's not even Wonderdick anymore. He's Stupid Ass-faced Hairy-Ball-Sack-Gargler Dick."

"That's a good one. Wordy, but good." She laughs, flipping her hand over to return the friendly squeeze. "But I'm not giving up, Dee. As soon as I get the sad out of my system, I'm getting back out there. There are wonderful men in the world, and if I keep my eyes open, I'm going to find one."

"Hell yes, you are," I agree. "And you don't even have to keep your eyes open. Just keep wearing shirts like that one, and the boobs will do the work for you."

She rolls her eyes. "You overestimate the power of cleavage."

"I do not. The bartender trips over his feet every time you so much as glance his way. And the guys with the faux-hawks have been drooling into their chip basket since we sat down."

"What's up with that I wonder?" She casts a glance over her shoulder to where two otherwise attractive guys have done their best to uglify themselves with faux-hawks, neon green and yellow T-shirts, and obnoxiously patterned pants.

"It's 80s night at the club across the street," the overly attentive bartender offers, materializing from nowhere with two fresh margaritas. "And these are from the suits near the window." He leans closer as he wipes a damp spot near our chip basket. "But between us, I wouldn't give them the time of day. One of them just slipped off his wedding ring and the other never tips."

"Monsters," Amanda says with a gasp, making the bartender grin. "Thank you for the warning, but we're having a girl date, so we're safe."

"You should check out 80s night, then." He nods toward the glass windows behind us. "Ladies get in free until ten."

"Oh, I haven't been dancing in years," Amanda demurs, fluttering her lashes at Cute Bartender. With his nut-brown skin and thickly-lashed brown eyes, he's the kind of adorable that could help a girl forget about her Wonderdick of an ex for a night, no doubt about that.

But when I softly suggest that I could get lost so Amanda can pick up a rebound guy, she shakes her head firmly. "No. Tonight is about convincing you that the angels are going to win."

I arch a brow. "Excuse me?"

"We're all born with our angels and demons already inside of us," Amanda says, pointing her skinny black straw at my chest. "From day one, they're fighting a war for the fate of our souls. If you give up hope and dump this guy you're crazy about because you're scared of something that hasn't happened yet—and might never happen—then the devils are going to win a big battle, baby. And then they're going to get cocky and start gunning for even more territory, bigger wins, until one morning you'll wake up and not recognize your own reflection in the mirror."

My lips turn down hard at the edges. "That's a terrible story."

"It's not a story," Mandy says, gaze unwavering. "It's what happened to my dad. I watched him become someone I didn't know anymore. Someone I didn't want to know, because his hopelessness destroyed everyone and everything he touched."

"I'm sorry," I say, my frown deepening. I don't remember much about Mandy's dad—he was an every-other-weekend parent by the time we were in middle school and had all but disappeared by the time we graduated—but I've heard the horror stories.

"Don't be sorry," she says. "Be better. Be tough. Jump into the deep end and swim like hell, and know that you have people who love you waiting to jump in and fish you out if the water gets too wild."

"How would pool water get wild?" I push away my third margarita, sensing that more hard liquor in my current fragile state would be a bad idea.

"Hurricane," Mandy offers. "Tornado. Earthquake. It doesn't matter. You know what I mean, and that's what I want you to think about tonight while we're walking like an Egyptian and living on a prayer."

I sit up straighter with an excited squee, clapping my hands together. "Really? We're going dancing? You're going to dance with me for once in your shy-about-dancing-in-public life?"

"Can't ask you to go out on a limb without being willing to crawl out there myself, can I?" She winks over the rim of her margarita glass. "Just let me finish getting drunk enough not to care what a bad dancer I am, then we'll go shake our groove thing."

"You're an incredible dancer." I wrap my arms around

her, leaning my lightly spinning head on her shoulder. "And I love you so much."

"I love you, too, lightweight," she says with a laugh.

"Am not," I say, wrinkling my nose. But by the time we get into the club, I'm feeling no pain. After another beer and an hour of dancing, the entire room is spinning. I dimly recall trying to fall asleep on a bench near the DJ booth and Amanda asking me if I mind if she stays out later—to spend time with some dude she met—and me agreeing that this was an excellent plan.

There are flashes of Amanda settling me in a cab and threatening the cabbie with dismemberment if I don't get home safely.

Not long after, I stumble up the stairs to my brother's house, where he and Laura laugh at me for being tipsy before ten o'clock on a Thursday and promise to get Amanda settled in the other guest room when she gets home.

And then I'm falling into bed with sloppily brushed teeth, while angels and demons swoop in circles around my head, waiting to see which way the battle is going to turn.

CHAPTER TWENTY-FOUR

From the texts of Amanda Esposito
and Diana Daniels

DIANA: Amanda? Where are you?

Please tell me you're downstairs having breakfast with my brother and Laura, even though your car isn't in the driveway...

FIVE MINUTES LATER...

DIANA: Amanda, please text me. I'm worried, but incapable of going to look for you because I have the worst hangover headache in the entire world.

This is why pot is so much better than booze.

Pot never makes me feel like my brain is being sliced and diced by a rusty blender installed at the base of my skull.

Also, my neck is probably broken.

Or at least it feels broken.

What did we do last night that could have resulted in a broken neck? I confess, it's all fuzzy after we decided 80s night was a good idea.

Please text me. ASAP.

Ten minutes later...

Diana: Dude, where are you? I dragged my pitiful, poisoned body downstairs to the kitchen, but you weren't there.

Nor are you anywhere else in the house, and no one saw your car pull out this morning, which I assume means you never came home. Did you go home with that hot guy you were staying to flirt with at the club?!

Was it fun?

Are you still asleep because you had so much fun?

I hope you are just asleep somewhere, snoozing off the fun…

Six minutes later...

Diana: OMG WHERE ARE YOU? Text me!

If you decided your trip to Portland wouldn't be complete without a one-night stand with a sexy stranger, you know I'm not going to judge. I just need to be sure Stranger hasn't chopped you into little pieces and buried you in his backyard.

Please call me.

Or text if you can't call.

I need to know you're okay.

Three minutes later...

Diana: If I don't hear from you by ten a.m., I'm calling the police.

I would rather freak out and realize later that there was no need to lose my shit than wait too long and regret it for the rest of my life.

If you end up getting hurt because you drove up here to cheer me up, I'm never going to forgive myself, Amanda.

I'm so sorry.

I never should have left you there alone.

I should have insisted you get in the cab with me, no matter how much the world was spinning.

Amanda: Shh, quiet...

Everything's okay.

Just hush for a second, all right?

Diana: You're okay! Thank God!

What do you mean hush for a second?

Amanda: Too much dinging...

I'm trying to sneak out of this house without getting caught, but you're making so much noise with the dinging. And more dinging. Ding, ding, ding.

DIANA: Dude. Turn your phone to silent.
Voila, no more dinging.

AMANDA: Shit. Yeah.
Okay. It's off.

DIANA: Are you still drunk?

AMANDA: No! Ugh, I don't know. I don't think so.
I think I'm just exhausted. I only slept an hour, maybe two at most.

DIANA: Because you were up all night banging your sexy stranger?

AMANDA: God... I'm so mortified...

DIANA: Don't be! There's nothing wrong with two consenting adults having a good time. I assume he showed you a good time and wasn't a selfish jerk who wouldn't go down on you.

AMANDA: You know I don't like to talk gritty details.

DIANA: But you will, as soon as you get back here and I can

ply you with caffeine and sugar until you crack under my enhanced interrogation techniques.

AMANDA: I won't crack. Not this time.

DIANA: That's what they all say…
warms up chocolate croissants
makes French press coffee that smells so good it will give your nose an orgasm to rival all the orgasms Sexy Stranger gave you last night

AMANDA: I can only remember about half the night, Diana.
And even that is kind of fuzzy. I was way more wasted than I thought. If I didn't know better, I would swear someone had put something in my drink.

DIANA: I think those margaritas were just really, REALLY strong.
I haven't been this hungover since I was in college, and I only had two of them and one beer. I'm sorry you can't remember if you had fun or not.
sad face emoji
And I'm sorry I abandoned you when you were in need of a keeper. I feel terrible.

AMANDA: It's not your fault. You were worse off than I was, and I'm the one who forced you into a cab and ran back into the club.
And I don't regret Sexy Stranger…

What I can recall of my time with him was…most enjoyable.

DIANA: So he went down on you?

AMANDA: For hours.
Like an Olympic champion of cunnilingus.

DIANA: Hell yeah, Sexy Stranger!

AMANDA: I think he may actually be an Olympic athlete. I have vague memories of discussing something sports-related, and he has a hint of a Russian accent that's sexy as math.

DIANA: Not my first choice of sexy things, but whatever floats your boat, girl.

AMANDA: He floated it. No doubt about that.
Even with a hangover, I feel better this morning than I have in a long time.
Just relaxed and happy and hopeful about a future with no Wonderdick in it.

DIANA: Awesome! I'm so happy for you!
And I knew I would get the sex scoop sooner or later…
devil emoji

Amanda: Fine. You're right. I always crack under pressure. But I still want coffee and pastries when I get there.

Diana: Are you going to see him again?
Give him a chance to rock your world while you're sober?

Amanda: Of course not! Are you crazy?
I'm sneaking out while he's still passed out cold, as the good Lord intended.

Diana: I know I'm a godless heathen, but I feel like I would know if "Thou shalt slink away in quiet shame post one-night stand" were actual scripture.

Amanda: It might as well be. There's no way this guy and I are going to have anything in common in real life. He's crazy athletic, dangerously gorgeous, and his house is big enough to fit ten of my apartment inside it and still have room left over. Not to mention that his driveway is so long I'm starting to have flashbacks to that time you made me hike for miles and miles into the woods with no food or water.

Diana: It was a mile-long trail, mostly flat.
A baby trail that never hurt anyone in its life.

Amanda: It hurt me. It made me very thirsty.

Oh, there's my car! Thank God. He said he was going to have someone pick it up and bring it here, but I wasn't sure if that promise ever became a legit plan.

DIANA: So he's gorgeous, athletic, wealthy, thoughtful, and a person who keeps promises, even after having had a few too many, but you're still running out of there as fast as your hung-over legs can carry you? Please tell me you at least got his number so you can call him when you come to your senses.

AMANDA: No. I don't have his, he doesn't have mine, and that's the way I like it.
I enjoyed the fireworks, but now it's morning and I have a friend to finish cheering up. Be there in fifteen, okay?

DIANA: Okay. But at least write down his address? Pretty please?
You never know when you might change your mind…

AMANDA: Does this mean you've changed yours?

DIANA: My head hurts too much to make serious decisions right now.
But I've been thinking a lot about our talk.
And thinking you might have made some solid points…

AMANDA: OMG, he has a Russian nesting doll for a mailbox.

DIANA: Really? That's pretty adorable…

AMANDA: It really is.

DIANA: Are you writing down his address?

AMANDA: No, I'm driving. Good-bye.

DIANA: *crying face* *loudly crying face* *cat crying face*

AMANDA: Your drama won't work here, woman.
   I've made my call. Now it's time to make yours.

CHAPTER TWENTY-FIVE

DIANA

I manage to get down the stairs to the kitchen without crawling this time, so I figure it's safe to consume liquids and grab a kombucha from the fridge then head out to the front porch. There my niece, Chloe, is playing with her pet hedgehog, Mr. Prickly Pants, in the shade while Brendan and Laura poke around in their raised vegetable beds on the far side of the front yard.

"Hey, Squirt," Chloe says, grinning up at me.

"No," I say for the thousandth time. "You do not get to call me Squirt. At least not until you're taller than me, like everyone else."

"I'm already halfway there. Won't be long now." Chloe giggles as Mr. Prickly Pants noses the toilet paper roll she's placed in front of him, sending it lolling across the porch. "Isn't Prickly Pants the cutest?"

"He is. I want to eat his face he's so cute." I take a sip of my drink and sag into the wicker loveseat. "Your dad giving you a break from being the designated weed puller today?"

"Yeah," Chloe says, tailing her pet on her hands and knees.

"He and Mom are having romantic morning time, so I get to hang out with Prickly instead."

My eyes widen, but I'm careful to keep my tone casual as I ask, "So you're calling Laura 'Mom' now?"

"Yeah." Chloe's private grin is so sweet and happy it breaks my heart a little. "She said I could."

"That's great, kiddo," I say, throat tight. "Laura really loves you."

"I know," she says matter of factly, making me think, not for the first time, that it must be nice to be Chloe.

Even when I was a kid, I can't remember trusting that I deserved good things the way she does. I was fearless with adventures of the body, but voyages of the heart were more carefully considered. I've always sort of assumed people weren't interested in liking me until they proved otherwise, rather than vice versa.

"Wonder why," I murmur, kneading the sore, broken-feeling place in my neck with my thumb, beginning to recall some poorly executed head-banging to "Back in Black."

"Wonder why what?" Chloe catches the toilet paper before it tumbles off the edge of the porch and redirects her hedgehog on a return roll.

"Nothing. Just thinking out loud."

"I wasn't sure at first," Chloe says, making my muddled brain work to follow the conversation. "But I talked to Dad, and he said my real mom wouldn't mind. He said she loved me so much that anything that made me happy would make her happy. And calling Laura Mom makes me happy. So I decided to do it without waiting until after the wedding. Why wait for something you want, when you can have it right now?" Chloe reaches for a box of dominos by my feet, pinning me with those luminous, wiser-than-her-years green eyes. "Because you never know how long you're going to get,

Aunt Dee. There's no time to waste. Especially for the good stuff."

I nod as the hairs lift on my arms and that "someone walked over my grave" sensation flutters through my bones. It's crazy, but it feels like the universe dropped a truth bomb on me, right out of the mouth of this eight-year-old girl. This kid who has somehow managed to stay fearless even after losing her mother when she was practically a baby.

"You're one of the bravest people I know, Chloe," I say softly.

She shoots me a "what have you been smoking" look that makes me laugh.

"Seriously," I insist. "You're brave and smart, and I want to be like you when I grow up."

"Thanks, I guess," she says with a shrug. "But I'm super afraid of seagulls. Just thinking about them makes me get sweaty all over and feel like I'm going to be sick." She studies me with a critical look. "And I'm pretty sure you're already grown up."

I pat her red curls fondly. "I'm glad you're only pretty sure."

"Well, you're short. And you're sillier than most grown-ups I know."

"True." I nod. "This is solid evidence. Maybe you'll be a lawyer when you grow up. Or a scientist. Or a therapist."

"I'm not sure I would be good at any of those things."

"You would be," I assure her. "Trust me."

She grins. "Okay. But I think I'm going to be a hedgehog breeder and an artist and a professional bike rider."

"That sounds lovely." I lean down, pressing an impulsive kiss to her cheek. "Thank you for the chat. Can you tell Amanda I'm upstairs when she gets here? I have something important I need to start working on right away."

"Sure. What is it? Can I help?"

I start to say no, but then experience a lightning storm of creative inspiration and point an enthusiastic finger at Chloe's chest. "Actually you can. You and Mr. Prickly Pants both. Meet me in your room by the costume trunk in ten minutes."

Chloe claps her hands. "Are we going to play dress-up?"

"We are," I say, chest fizzing with a potent mixture of hope and daring. "And make some art, too. And maybe a little magic while we're at it."

CHAPTER TWENTY-SIX

TANNER

The world can be a hard, ugly place filled with bitter, selfish people.

But every once in a while, you get a reminder of how incredible life can be when someone is willing to go above and beyond the call of duty for a friend.

Or an ex-boyfriend, in this case...

I sent off my emails last night, assuming most of my old flames wouldn't bother to write back, and those who did wouldn't be in any hurry about it. Why should they when they have lives, spouses, careers, and/or kids making demands far higher on their priority list than a blast from the past?

But to my surprise, I wake up Friday morning with five responses waiting in my inbox. A sixth pops up while I'm printing out the first batch, and by ten a.m. I'm in possession of seven letters of reference.

Seven of the women I dated still like me enough to encourage the woman I'm falling in love now with to give me a chance at her heart.

I've always tried to be a good boyfriend, a decent ex, and

a forgiving person when someone I care about lets me down, and this feels like a sign that I'm on the right path. I'm living a life I can be proud of, and I've got hard evidence that I am who I say I am, someone whose strengths and weaknesses are laid out in plain sight, with no hidden agenda or evil master plan.

I'm not like the losers Diana has dated, and I'm going to prove it to her.

Today. Immediately, in fact.

As soon as I can find a way to convince her to talk to me...

I'm considering my options, wondering if sending flowers accompanied by an envelope containing my reference letters will be enough to convince Diana to read them, when Wanda squeals loudly from the patch of shade near the back gate. I sit up in the hammock and glance over my shoulder to see her trotting quickly around the side of the house, tail wiggling and a pink envelope in her mouth, which she carries past me to the pool and promptly drops into the sparkling blue water.

"No! Bad pig." I leap out of the hammock to rescue the envelope before it's destroyed. Thankfully, it's made of thick card stock, sturdy enough to protect the card within.

As soon as I see the image on the front of the card—a photograph of Wanda wearing the flowered bikini my sister ordered for her and an "I refuse to apologize for how cute I am" expression—I know who this is from. On impulse, I jog over to the gate and push it open, hurrying out to the sidewalk to scan the street, but there's no sign of Diana.

She must have dropped the card and dashed.

Cursing under my breath for not being faster, I open the card with a mixture of hope and dread that morphs into cautious optimism as I read the simple note within—

You're right.

We should talk in person.
Meet me at sunset on the beach where we first met?
I've got something I need to show you.
Sincerely,
Diana

I read it three times, chewing my bottom lip as I debate the possible implications of such a meeting. Surely, if she intended to call us off once and for all, she wouldn't have picked the place where we shared our first make-out session as our meeting spot. Unless, of course, she's bringing me back there to remind me how firmly she tried to shut down any possible avenues into romance from the very start.

But that would be cruel, and Diana isn't the kind to rub salt in a wound.

Rubbing salt in a wound creates an antibacterial environment that helps it heal faster, my inner voice helpfully supplies. Maybe Diana thinks swift, intense pain will be easier for you than a softer, gentler pain that drags on for months while you slowly get it through your thick head that you're never going to wake up next to her beautiful, sexy, naked body and sunshine smile ever again.

"Fuck that," I mutter aloud.

That's not going to happen. Diana and I aren't through, not by a long shot. I have no idea what she has planned for this evening, but I plan on making some very compelling arguments of my own for her moving back in with me.

I spend the rest of the day arming myself for battle. I bike down to the office store a few blocks over and have my reference letters bound into a small booklet, professional presentation style. Back at home, I shower, shave, manscape, and anoint myself with the various lotions and creams I know

Diana likes best and dress in jeans and a white dress shirt with the sleeves rolled up. It's still hot in the city, but on the coast, it will be cool and get cooler after the sun goes down.

I spend the drive west listening to the Pandora channel Diana got me hooked on—the Shins mixed with the Beatles—and going over what I plan to say.

Tonight, I don't struggle to keep my mind on the matter at hand. My focus is laser sharp and every cell in my body is humming with a single, united purpose—to get her back.

I have to get her back. We're only a few weeks into being together, but it's already clear that this is different than anything that's come before. Diana is different, special, the kind of person who sweeps into your life and makes you wonder how you ever thought you were complete without her.

My head fills with feelings, wishes, and memories of Diana's smile, and by the time I find a parking spot and swing out into the cool coastal air, I'm carrying more than a booklet full of references. I'm carrying every choice I've made while figuring out how to be in love, and every lesson I've learned on my way to becoming a person I'm proud of. I make mistakes and fuck up my fair share, but I'm not my father or the assholes who broke my mom's heart when I was little and she was on her own with three kids and no one to help her hold our family together.

And I'm not the liars who made Diana afraid to trust something that feels this right, either.

I'm carrying a big load, but it doesn't feel heavy. I've never felt lighter or more certain that I'm where I'm supposed to be, fighting for what's right.

I'm so ready to see Diana—and dive right into the battle for us—that when I arrive at the sheltered corner of the beach to find nothing but a folding table with a small black piece of electronic equipment sitting on it, I can't help feeling deflated.

I turn, scanning the coast and the cliff rising above me on the right, but there's no sign of Dee. The only other out of the ordinary thing about this sleepy summer beach scene is a white sheet someone has secured to the face of the cliff, which I hadn't noticed at first. Brow furrowing, I move closer to the folding table and see a note taped to the top of a small, portable projector.

"Please press play," it reads.

Tucking my booklet beneath my arm, I hit the play button and lift my gaze to the white sheet. The sun is still barely visible above the waves, but it's dark enough for me to see the old-fashioned countdown that flickers onto the sheet, followed by a title sequence that reads:

Confessions of a Love-A-Holic
  A Daniels and Daniels film
  Produced in Portland
  Starring Chloe Daniels as Tanner Nowicki
  And Prickly Pants the hedgehog as Diana Daniels

I grin as Chloe appears on the screen dressed in a Badgers jersey with her hair tucked up in a ball cap and fake whiskers drawn on her face. She props her hands on her hips and talks earnestly to someone off screen. There's no sound, but subtitles have been helpfully provided, so I know "Tanner" is saying, "Talk to me, Diana. All I'm asking is that we have an adult discussion about why you ended this via email. Is that too much to ask?"

The next shot is of a hedgehog dressed in a tiny white sundress, rolling a roll of toilet paper across what looks like the top of a bookcase. "I'm sorry," the Diana hedgehog says via subtitles. "Hedgehogs are naturally shy, timid, defensive creatures."

Chloe rolls her eyes with an eloquence that makes subtitling unnecessary.

"Fine!" The hedgehog stands on its hind legs, nose wiggling. "So I'm not shy or timid, but I am defensive. I've spent a decade rolling from one bad relationship into an even worse one, like an addict headed for rock bottom. And sure, I can blame some of it on bad luck, but I have to take my share of the blame, too." The hedgehog's tongue slips out, delicately probing her own nostrils in a way that's funny, gross, and heart-wrenching at the same time. Though it's the words on the bottom of the screen, not the hedgehog's antics, that are making my pulse race. "I've always seen what I wanted to see in someone new, instead of what's actually there. I think I'm finally seeing someone clearly, but how can I trust myself? And why should I believe this is the moment when things turn around?"

"Why shouldn't you believe it?" Chloe asks, folding her arms at her chest. "Slavery ended. Women got the vote. Eventually Vin Diesel will be too old to make action flicks, and we'll all be spared another Fast and the Furious movie. Justice does occasionally win out in the end. More than occasionally, if people are willing to give it a hand."

Hedgehog Diana waddles in a circle, looking spiny and uncomfortable in her dress. "But what if it's a long time before I'm ready to relax my quills and trust in justice, Tanner? How can I ask you to put up with me being a stress case when you're obviously an emotionally healthy human ready to give and receive healthy human feelings, and I'm a nervous, prickly insectivore?"

My grin fades.

I'm totally willing to wait for Dee to be ready for a healthy human relationship, a truth I'm relieved to see echoed by my on-screen self when Chloe rests her fake-whiskered chin on her fist and says, "And what if I say I'm happy to wait? Is that going to be the end of the running and excuses?"

The camera cuts to a shot of hedgehog-Diana running in figure eights on the carpet, her white dress flapping, which is cute, but not reassuring to real life me. Or to on-screen me, apparently, since the next shot is a close-up of Chloe narrowing her eyes and slowly lifting a thin red brow.

Cut to the hedgehog running some more.

Cut back to Chloe wiggling her eyebrows in a way that reminds me more of Diana than myself, but is even cuter than the hedgehog.

Cut to the hedgehog falling over and rolling into a ball, the white dress trapped beneath it like the cape of a fallen superhero.

Cut to a heavy sigh from Chloe as she lies down on the carpet next to the hedgehog, her face slowly coming into focus as the rolled up ball in the foreground goes blurry. "It's not a hard question," Chloe says in what I can tell is a gentle voice. The kid has a future in acting. I hardly need to glance at the subtitles to know exactly what Chloe-Tanner is feeling. "And I don't think I deserve to be cast as the bad guy because I dared to ask it. Do you?"

Cut to the Diana hedgehog sitting in a muffin tin, looking very muffin-like surrounded by actual muffins the same light brown as her quills.

I laugh, wondering what the hell the muffin tin has to do with anything, then laugh harder when Chloe props her hands on her hips and says, "Quit trying to change the subject," and Diana hedgehog sheepishly says, "Just trying to remind you that my muffin top brings all the boys to the yard. I do have some good qualities, you know."

Chloe nods thoughtfully.

"But in all seriousness," Diana hedgehog says, now sitting on Chloe's shoulder, nuzzling her neck. "If you think you can handle taking it slow, I'll try my best not to run, and to realize that you're not the latest in a long line of anything. You're you. Only you. And you have never been anything but wonderful to me."

Cut to a close-up of the hedgehog looking cranky in a tiny red hammock. "Except that time you threatened to take down my yoga swing."

I shake my head and admit, "Everyone makes mistakes," as the camera cuts back to the hedgehog snuggling Chloe's neck. The screen slowly fades to black, and the end credits roll:

Confessions of a Love-A-Holic was made possible by...

A hedgehog dress made by Chloe's grandmother...

A roll of toilet paper stolen from the downstairs bathroom...

A muffin tin on loan from the Daniels' kitchen...

A scrap of red fabric (as no hot-pink fabric was available)...

A Badgers jersey purchased at a home game when Chloe was six...

The acting talents of Chloe Daniels and Mr. Prickly Pants in the gender-bending roles sure to win them both Academy Award nominations, and in cooperation with The Society for Better Living through Learning to Trust People Who Seem Like They Might Want to Love You.

There's no might about it, I think, my throat going tight as

Diana slips out from behind a curve in the face of the cliff, a nervous expression on her face.

"Hey," she says, nibbling at her bottom lip. "Well, at least we made you laugh. That's a good thing."

"A very good thing." I stand my ground by the folding table, letting her come to me. "How are you?"

"I've been better." Her fingers tangle in front of her as she gestures down at the white sundress she's wearing. "Editing the movie took so long I didn't have time to iron my dress."

"Too bad. Because I only love you when your dresses are perfectly ironed."

Her eyes go wide, and she shakes her head, waving an arm toward the now-blank screen. "You don't have to say that, Tanner. I didn't mean—"

"I know what you meant," I cut in. "And you've got me pegged. I do want to love you. All I need is the green light."

Diana's eyes begin to shine. "How can you really be this great?"

"Because you're worth it, and you make me happy. And what other man can say his girl made him a silent movie apology starring a hedgehog in a dress?" I ask, grinning as Diana laughs.

"Mr. Prickly Pants is packing a lot of talent in that little body."

"So are you." I hold out a hand. "Now get over here so I can show you how grateful I am to be your boyfriend."

* * *

Diana

WHAT WOMAN in her right mind could resist an offer like that?

And I am in my right mind. As Tanner pulls me in for a

fiercely sweet hug that leaves no doubt how grateful he is to have me back where I belong, the last of my fear fades away. I know it won't all be smooth sailing, and there's a chance this roll of the dice will blow up in my face the way all the others have, but he's worth the risk. He's worth crawling out on that limb, because deep in my bones I sense this time it's not going to break.

"And you don't mind that I'm a little older?" I tilt my head back to gaze into his clear green eyes, which are looking even dreamier than usual in the warm sunset light.

He shoots me an "are you fucking kidding me?" look that makes me laugh.

"And you don't mind if I stay at Brendan's house for a while?" I ask, nose wrinkling. "So we can take it slow and know that we're moving in together for the right reasons? I'm still happy to watch Wanda any time you need help, I just…want to handle us with care."

"Sounds good. I like being handled with care," he says, before adding in a softer voice. "Though I hope you'll still sleep over every once in a while."

"Hell yes, I'm sleeping over." I huff incredulously. "How else are we going to have time to figure out how to bang in my yoga swing?"

He grins. "How did you know I've been dying to bang in the yoga swing?"

"You're easy to read." I press up on tiptoe, bringing my lips closer to his. "It's one of the things I'm starting to love about you."

He hugs me tighter. "Starting is good."

"It is," I agree, my pulse picking up as his hand cups my bottom, pulling me closer to where he's harder, thicker than he was a moment before. "Finishing is good, too. So what do you say we take this to the hotel room I booked? It's just on the other side of the bluff. We can be there in five minutes if we hurry."

He makes a husky, appreciative sound low in his throat. "Have I told you lately how brilliant you are?"

"No. But I wasn't very brilliant for a while there. I'm sorry."

"No more apologies. It's in the past." He kisses me with a tenderness that makes my heart melt. "And I'm only interested in the future. The very near future, in particular, when I'm going to have you out of this dress and coming on my mouth."

"That sounds very nice," I whisper.

And it is very nice.

And lovely. And sexy. And right…

From the moment we close the door to our room overlooking the ocean to the next morning when I wake up in Tanner's arms, the place where I hope to keep waking up in for many, many mornings to come.

EPILOGUE

TANNER

Three months later...

WHAT'S that they say about the best-laid plans?

That they're stupid, useless, and futile? Because the moment you make a plan something—fate, karma, or simply the worst team in the NHL—starts plotting to put your plan through the shredder, making you wish you had learned your lesson about taking things for granted.

"What the fuck?" Petrov kicks the boards in front of us, causing a few unattended water bottles to tumble to the floor. "Where the hell is this coming from? They're the worst team in the league."

"And they're kicking our collective asses," Justin grumbles from farther down the bench, clearly itching to get back on the ice.

What was supposed to be a shut-out has turned into a nail-biter. For years, the sweet southern bastards we're playing have been the jokes of the NHL. Chaos is their stock in trade, and I've never seen a more disorganized offense or flailing defense.

And they're still scrambling and flailing today, but for some reason, lady luck is on their side. Shots that seem to be going wide ricochet off our own players to end up in our net, bumbling defense attempts are somehow thwarting our forwards, and the sweet southern goalie has chosen today to stop sucking and start earning his keep.

This is about as far as possible from the easy, breezy win I was expecting, and I'm beginning to wish Diana and I had chosen another night to spring a surprise wedding on our nearest and dearest. I don't care if we lose—well, yes, I care, but I'm so excited to be marrying Diana in less than an hour, I know I'll snap back from the post-game blues pretty quick —but I'm not looking forward to a wedding party full of pissed off, cranky Badgers.

We have to win this. That's it.

We've got to get out there, break this tie, and kick ass in the third period so my friends can enjoy my wedding, damn it.

"This is chaos, plain and simple. This isn't anything we can't handle," I say, raising my voice to be heard over the groan of the Badger fans behind us as our forwards ring another shot off the goal post. "These douchebags are getting lucky, but we actually have a clean, efficient game. We just need to sharpen our focus and cut through the bullshit."

"Great pep talk, rookie," Justin grumbles.

"Thanks, but I'm not finished." I force a smile. "Their defensemen are leaving their positions without support. If we keep things sharp and elegant out there, those fuckers won't know what hit them."

"Sharp and elegant, huh?" Justin arches a brow. "When did you become such a classy bastard?"

"He's right," Petrov says, motioning toward the ice. "Their

forwards aren't covering for the defense. If we chip the puck to center ice for an odd man break and keep it elegant, we'll break the tie. Keep it up in the third, and we get to go have a beer after it's all over and not feel like assholes for handing a game to a bunch of minor leaguers."

Brendan, who's been quiet up to this point, nods. "Let's do it. As soon as Coach calls our line."

Our line. I'm playing first line for the first time this game—another reason I would really prefer not to leave the ice holding my ass.

Thirty seconds later, Coach Swindle barks for us to "change 'em up," and Justin, Brendan, and I jump over the boards.

We line up for the face-off and lose to the Sweet Southern Bastards, who dump the puck into our zone and bound away after it like so many slobbering golden retrievers. But Petrov, a man who has no love for animals, crushes their perky puck carrier against the boards with a crash that rattles the glass, then steals the puck and shoots it around to where I'm waiting, ready to exit the zone.

As we'd hoped, the Southern defense rushes my position, abandoning their posts without hesitation, while I cut hard to the left, then loft the puck toward center ice.

Sweet, nearly empty center ice...where Justin is wide open to scoop up the gift I've delivered and haul ass toward the goal. He's moving fast, but I've been running every other morning with Adams for two months, and in seconds I catch up to him, riding his skates the last few yards to the goal. Brendan is behind us, occupying the lone defender who's managed to get his ass back on this side of the centerline, so we're free and clear to bring this home.

Justin walks in on the goalie, faking to the right as he knocks the puck to the left, right into my waiting stick. And then, like a doctor delivering breech twins, I slip the puck expertly into the net to score.

Okay, it's nothing like delivering twins, but it feels so fucking good. And as the crowd erupts into howls of victory, I swear I can hear my beach pixie hooting her unique war cry.

I glance up, spotting Diana jumping up and down and cheering like a crazy person next to Chloe and Laura. She waves congratulations, and I blow her a kiss, which she pretends to catch and pop into her mouth like an invisible bon-bon.

I laugh, prompting a slap on the back from Petrov.

"Don't get too comfortable," he says. "We need to keep the pressure up going into the third."

"We will," I say, skating back to center ice beside him. "And once we're four or five points ahead, remind me to ask you an important question."

Petrov shoots me a narrow look but doesn't push the issue. That's one of the things I've come to appreciate about Petrov in the past few months. When Justin was warning me not to let Diana move back in so soon—only two weeks after she moved out, because who were we kidding, we couldn't stand being apart—and Brendan was giving me the stink eye every time Diana showed up after practice to surprise me with takeout or tickets to a movie or a mannequin wrapped in a cocoon of yarn that we tied to Justin's car to congratulate him on a new endorsement deal with a national crafting store, Petrov kept his thoughts to himself. He'd offered his two cents a long time ago and was content to let events play out without any meddling on his part.

That's why I'm going to ask him to be my best man.

Well, that, and because Diana is going to ask Brendan to be her maid of honor, just to see if she can get him to wear a tiara, because my future wife isn't taking our wedding too seriously. The decision to get married was something we talked about a lot, but once the decision was made, we just wanted to get hitched as quickly, easily, and enjoyably as possible so we can get started on the happily ever after.

We head into the third period like evil robots sent to clean up the mess some primitive civilization has left behind. We give no quarter, we show no mercy, and by the time the buzzer sounds, we've spanked the Southern Bastards seven to four and given the fans something to cheer about.

Back in the locker room, evidence of Diana's handiwork is hanging from the locker of every member of the team. Justin is the first to rip open his invite, making me nervous until a smile bursts across his face. "Aw, Nowicki! You're growing up so fast!"

"Congratulations," Brendan says, with an only slightly less enthusiastic smile. "Diana told me about the plan this morning. She wanted to give me an early heads-up in case I decided to have a shit fit about it."

I nod with a nervous laugh. "So how did that go?"

"Small shit fit," he says, grin widening. "But I'm happy for you. She loves you a lot."

"I love her, too. More than anything. I promise I won't ever give you a reason to regret standing up with us today."

His breath rushes out. "I doubt that, since I'm sure Diana is going to get some pictures of me in that damned tiara, but a man can hope."

Forty-five minutes later, up in a sky box decorated like a stretch of Oregon coastline complete with seagull and wave sound effects supplied by my lovely bride, surrounded by the men who are my on-ice family and the amazing people who will become part of my newly extended family, I say my vows to the most beautiful, sexy, perfect woman in the world.

"I know some people don't go in for love at first sight." I

cast Petrov, who looks more anxious about being best man than I expected him to be, a narrow glance before shifting my attention back to Dee. "But a part of me knew I was going to fall in love with you that first night on the beach, when you warned me about the killer mermaids. You are by far the most unique person I've ever met. You're special in ways I didn't know existed before I met you, and I can't believe I'm the lucky bastard who gets to share the rest of his life with you. You make me so happy, Beach Pixie, and I've never been more excited than this moment, right now, when I get to promise you forever."

Diana sucks in a breath, pressing her lips together before shaking her head. "Damn it, I knew you were going to make me cry."

Our friends and family laugh, the sound giving Diana the moment she needs to regain her composure.

When she does, she squeezes my hands, looking up at me with a mixture of love and faith so intense it makes the rest of the world fade away. "Tanner Nowicki, I've never met anyone as patient, kind, and quietly gifted at being a truly lovely person as you are. Every day, in every way, you adore me in a fashion I'm not sure I deserve." She sniffs. "Except maybe I do, because I adore you right back. You are everything I want and everything I'm ever going to need. And if agreeing to take on a last name like Nowicki for the next forty or fifty years doesn't prove I love you to distraction, I don't know what will." Her eyes suddenly widen as she glances over her shoulder to add, "Sorry, Nowickis in the room."

"That's okay, sis." Chey, who's joining us via Skype, pipes up from the laptop my mom is holding. "I'm the only one who hasn't married out of the name, and I'm on that as soon as possible."

There's more laughter, and then a few words from Jax,

who graciously agreed to put his ordained-to-marry status to use for Diana and me tonight, and then I get to kiss my bride.

And call me crazy, but I swear the kiss tastes different than the one I stole before we walked down the aisle together ten minutes ago. It's sweeter, sexier, and serious in a way that isn't the least bit scary.

At least not for me…

"Happy?" I mouth as we pull back from the kiss.

"So happy. Though one thing could make me happier," she says, adding in a louder voice, "Wanda come!"

She's answered by a high-pitched squeal from the back of the room. I look back to see Wanda, dressed in a pig-sized flower-girl dress, trotting down the aisle with an envelope in her mouth. This time, however, instead of depositing it in the nearest body of water, she drops it delicately at my feet.

"Good pig," I praise her, patting her flank as I fetch the envelope and stand, lifting a brow in Diana's direction.

"Open it," she says, grinning. "I think you're going to like what you see."

I open the envelope, pulling out two plane tickets to Bali.

"For three weeks next summer we'll be staying on a remote island in Indonesia," Diana says, looping her arm through mine. "Said to be the home of a race of killer mermaids whose tears are harvested for their healing powers!" She bounces lightly on her toes, her excitement so infectious I have to fight the urge to start bouncing with her. "Isn't that the most exciting thing ever? I mean, aside from the fact that we're married."

I kiss her forehead, smiling against her skin. "Yes. Aside from the fact that we're married, it's the most exciting thing ever."

"But you're not postponing the honeymoon that long." Laura pulls first Diana, and then me, in for a hug. "We're welcoming Tanner to the family with the keys to our cabin near Mount Hood."

"That's right." Brendan slips his arm around Laura. "We expect you to enjoy yourselves, drink all the champagne our housekeeper is putting in the fridge as we speak, and make lots of beautiful first-weekend-as-married-people memories."

Before I can thank Brendan and Laura, Justin and his fiancée Libby are taking their turn in the line of well-wishers, Justin giving me shit for beating him to the altar and Libby wiping away tears and swearing the vows were so beautiful she could hardly stand it. The next two hours are filled with laughs, a few tears, dancing, drinking, cake eating, and quick good-byes as the staff tells us they really can't keep the box open another minute.

Somewhere in the madness, Diana loses her best friend (and second maid of honor), Amanda, but a quick text confirms that Mandy is alive and on her way to her new apartment, not far from the arena, and Diana and I head for home.

I'm beat from the game and exhausted from the emotional toll of the wedding, but the moment we close the door behind us and get Wanda tucked into her pen for the night, the tiredness fades, replaced by the all-consuming need to get my wife into bed.

"Upstairs," I whisper into her hair, my fingers finding the zipper on her white satin dress and pulling it down. "I need to consummate this marriage, Diana Nowicki."

She guides my mouth to hers, kissing me in the near darkness. "We're going to consummate the shit out this marriage."

I smile against her lips. "Hell yes, we are. So get your ass upstairs before I take you right here and scar the poor pig for life."

"Heaven forbid." With a giggle, Diana turns, racing up the stairs, slipping out of her dress on the top landing, and ditching her bra halfway to the master bedroom. By the time we reach the bed, she's naked, and we tumble onto the sheets, working together to get my tux out of our way.

"I love you," Diana whispers as we fumble with buttons and zippers. "I'm so happy to be your wife."

"Me, too. But I want to make you even happier." I kiss my way down her beautiful body, pausing to lick and tease her delicious nipples, making her squirm and sigh, before I continue my exploration.

I kiss her ribs, her belly, and each adorably knotty hipbone, before moving down to her damp curls. I urge her legs apart with my hands at the back of her knees, moaning in appreciation as she opens for me.

"Is your clit the most beautiful clit because I love you?" I murmur, spreading her with my fingers until there is nothing impeding my view of her sweet pink clit. "Or do I love you at least partly because of this jaunty little beauty?"

"You found me out." She shifts restlessly beneath me as her fingers tangle in my hair. "My clit has wizard powers."

"Enchantress powers," I correct. "No way is your clit a dude."

"Why? Are you bothered by the thought that you're kissing—" Her words end in a sharp intake of breath as my tongue sweeps up her center, through the well of heat at her entrance, to her clit, where I show her how not bothered I am by her sexy as sin body.

I lick and tease and fuck her with my mouth, exploring every inch of her pussy, finding all the places that only I know give her pleasure, the places we've discovered together in our mutual determination to take making love to places neither of us has been before.

And like every time with Diana, by the time she comes for

me the first time—bucking into my fingers while my tongue attends to her clit, flicking back and forth until she screams my name—I swear I can feel her pleasure pulsing inside my own skin. I'm a part of her, and she's a part of me, and knowing our forever is sealed with promises and the ring on my finger makes every moment even sweeter.

"Inside me," she breathes, tugging lightly on my ears. "Oh please, I need you inside me. Right now."

And because her wish is my command, and my pleasure, and my reason for being, I move over her, positioning my throbbing cock and pushing inside. I glide into her molten heat, slow and steady, thrusting forward until my balls pulse in the seam of her ass and I'm consumed by the certainty that I'm back where I belong.

"So perfect," she sighs, tongue dancing with mine as we begin to move together, advancing and retreating, playing this game that always ends in a victory for both sides.

"Beautiful." I circle my hips, making sure to nudge her clit at the end of each thrust. "And mine."

"Yours," she confirms, rocking her hips forward, taking me deeper. "And you are mine."

"Forever," I promise. "Until hedgehogs play hockey and pigs have wings and humans are a legend the mermaids sing about before they swim off to war."

Diana's eyes begin to shine. "You're a poet, Muscle Boy."

"Only with you, sweetness," I say, the tension building low in my body until I know I won't be able to hold on much longer. "Now will you allow me the pleasure of making you come for me again?"

"Oh yes, I'm there, I'm already there." She bucks into my cock, coating me with her slick heat, drawing me deeper into her body, her heart, her love so sweet that as I come I forget I'm just a man with a man's limitations, a man's faults, and a man's short time on this planet.

For a moment, with my wife holding me close as our bodies pulse with magic, I glimpse possibilities bigger and brighter than anything I could have imagined on my own.

"I want to do everything with you," I murmur against her neck.

"Yes," she agrees. "Everything is better with you. Especially coming. The coming is really top notch."

And because I'm a glutton for praise, I carry her into the bathroom and make her come again in the bath, with my fingers soaping her nipples as I take her from behind, getting her off seconds before the water rises high enough to reach where I'm thrusting inside her. Before morning we christen the floor by the bed, the wall beside the closet, and round out the consummating with some slow, languid missionary that ends in an orgasm so intense I would worry I've damaged myself, but I'm too drunk on Diana to care.

And when we wake up the next afternoon, stretching in the autumn sunshine streaming through the curtains, she's even more beautiful than she was before.

It doesn't seem possible, but it's true. And damn if she doesn't get more beautiful every day until, by the time we pack for our honeymoon eight months later, there is no doubt in my mind that I landed the prettiest woman in the world. Pretty on the outside, prettier on the inside, and, through some miraculous twist of fate, mine.

"I don't think I can get any happier," I murmur as we drift back and forth in an ocean-side hammock, watching the boat that delivered us to our quiet, nearly deserted Indonesian island chug away through the aquamarine waves.

"What if I told you this island is famous for something other than killer mermaids?" Diana asks, slipping a hand beneath my T-shirt.

"Something like what?"

"Apparently it was blessed by a fertility goddess." She slips the button on my shorts through the buttonhole. "Seems like a shame to waste that kind of magic, don't you think?"

I do. Hell yes, I do.

And by the time we leave three weeks later, with Diana's period already several days late, I am an even happier man.

Because the world is full of miracles.

And that is the truth. Don't let anyone tell you different.

Keep reading for an excerpt of
Puck Me Baby,
Petrov and Amanda's story.

TELL LILI YOUR FAVORITE PART!

I love reading your thoughts about the books and your review matters. Reviews help readers find new-to-them authors to enjoy. So if you could take a moment to leave a review letting me know your favorite part of the story—nothing fancy required, even a sentence or two would be wonderful—I would be deeply grateful.

ABOUT THE AUTHOR

Lili Valente has slept under the stars in Greece, eaten dinner at midnight with French men who couldn't be trusted to keep their mouths on their food, and walked alone through Munich's red light district after dark and lived to tell the tale.

These days you can find her writing in a tent beside the sea, drinking coconut water and thinking delightfully dirty thoughts.

You can find Lili on the web at...
www.lilivalente.com
lili.valente.romance@gmail.com

ALSO BY LILI VALENTE

Fall hard for Lili's SEXY flirty romantic comedies!
Magnificent Bastard
Spectacular Rascal
Incredible You
Meant for You
Learn more here

Master Me Series
Snowed in with the Boss
Masquerade with the Master
Very Dirty Billionaire
Learn more here

To the Bone Series
A Love so Dangerous
A Love so Deadly
A Love so Deep
Learn more here

Under His Command Series
Controlling Her Pleasure (Free!)
Commanding Her Trust
Claiming Her Heart
Learn more here

Bought by the Billionaire Series

Dark Domination (Free!)

Deep Domination

Desperate Domination

Divine Domination

Learn more here

Kidnapped by the Billionaire Series

Dirty Twisted Love (Free!)

Filthy Wicked Love

Crazy Beautiful Love

One More Shameless Night

Learn more here

Bedding the Bad Boy Series

The Bad Boy's Temptation (Free!)

The Bad Boy's Seduction

The Bad Boy's Redemption

Learn more here

SNEAK PEEK

SNEAK PEEK OF PUCK ME BABY COMING FALL 2017

Petrov

A Russian proverb says that falling in love is like a mouse falling into a box—there is no way out. That's it. Once you're in, you're trapped, a prisoner at the mercy of beings larger and more powerful than you, poor little mouse, will ever be.

My grandmother, a tiny babushka with the thick Russian accent of a 1980s movie villain, remembers every proverb she's ever heard.

Especially the ones about love.

Love is the reason she was married at fifteen and widowed at sixteen when her young husband was killed in a brawl outside her dormitory the night they had planned to steal away from Moscow. Love is the reason she defected from the Soviet Union, and her ballet company, during a tour of Paris when she fell for a charismatic French painter who would later leave her for a younger dancer when Baba was six-months pregnant.

Love is the reason she married a man from Seattle less

than a year later—this time for the love of her daughter, who she had vowed to provide with all the best things in life. And through twenty-eight years of marriage to the only grandfather I've ever known, she was a good and caring wife.

But she never loved him like a mouse falling into a box. She'd learned her lesson about that kind of love.

"Love will love a goat, my sunshine," Baba would warn me in hushed tones when I was small and my mother and father were fighting in the other room in French, the only language they spoke that I couldn't understand. "Love will kiss the goat's face and call it the most beautiful face in the world. Remember that, and look before you jump into the box. Better to be a good friend than a lovesick mouse."

Even at six, I understood the main thrust of her argument —my dad was a fucking loser goat my mother never should have kissed, a fact proven when dear old dad disappeared shortly before my seventh birthday, never to return, or pay a dime of child support.

But the rest of Baba's message took some living to sort out.

By the time I realized she was encouraging me to look for a long-term relationship based on friendship and mutual respect rather than passion, Renee had already lost the baby, blamed me for her pain, stolen the new car I'd bought Baba with my Badger signing bonus, and run off to Vegas to marry a Columbian drug lord she'd met at her Zumba class.

True story.

Apparently even Columbian drug lords enjoy dance-based cardio.

Since then, I've dated—even semi-seriously once or twice —but I've never landed in the box. I've danced around the edge of the box, stared at the shimmering floor far below, even leaned over to sniff the sweet air inside, but I've never fallen in.

Like Baba, I know better. The air may smell sweet, but it will eventually start to reek. And then the damned box will run out of oxygen, and I'll be trapped at the bottom, sucking air and praying for the love spell to break before I suffocate.

Needless to say, I'm not looking to get romantically involved. And even if I were, I know better than to pursue a woman simply because the sex was hot the one night we spent together. Yes, Mandy was fun, witty, wild, and a wet dream on the dance floor. Yes, she has melted-chocolate eyes, the kind of silky brown hair that makes my fingers itch to be buried in it, and a body that won't quit, but...

Shit...

That body, with the curves for miles, seriously won't quit.

And I can't quit stealing glances at the maid of honor over the heads of the couple getting hitched. That black dress with the plunging neckline shows off spectacular cleavage produced by her even more spectacular breasts. I'm supposed to be focused on my friend and teammate and the woman he's promising to love for the rest of his life, but I can't stop thinking about Amanda naked in my bed, calling my name as I made her come again and again while I devoured her pussy like a starving man given a jar of honey and a spoon.

She was delicious, addictive, and by far the sweetest, sexiest thing I'd laid hands on in longer than I could remember.

That night as we fell asleep tangled in sheets that smelled of her and me and all the fun we'd had, my alcohol-and-orgasm-buzzed brain had dared to think about something more. Something more than a night or a summer. Something more than casual dating or friends with benefits. After just a few hours, this woman had me at the edge of the box, leaning over so far I could have brushed the smooth, wooden floor with my fingertips.

There was something about her that spoke to something in me, and I was positive she felt it, too. So positive that when I woke up to find my bed empty and not so much as a note or a phone number left behind, I was certain I must have missed something. I searched every inch of the house, looking for a scrap of paper that had drifted beneath the bed or been blown under the couch by a morning breeze.

I even moved the refrigerator. Just in case.

But there was no note, no number, no sign that the girl with the suck-you-under-her-spell eyes wanted more than a one-night stand.

After a few days of waiting, hoping she would swing by to pick up the sunglasses she'd left in my car, I came to terms with the fact that I was never going to see her again, and put her out of my mind.

It was for the best, really. I was a month away from turning thirty, and starting to feel my age on the ice. The last thing I needed was a sexy distraction to blow my focus heading into my eighth season as a Portland Badger.

But now, here she is, less than three feet away, standing up at the wedding of our mutual friends. All this time, we've been one degree of separation from each other, poised for another inevitable run-in with the chemistry that flairs like flames drenched in kerosene every time our eyes meet.

As the man officiating the wedding pronounces Nowicki and Diana husband and wife, Amanda's gaze meets mine, locking and holding as I telegraph through the electrically-charged air—*We should talk. Don't you think?*

Oh dear, her eyes respond. *Yes. Maybe? This is complicated...*

My lips curve. *Only as complicated as we make it, mishka. We could think too hard and talk too much. Or you could come home with me and let me make you come all night long.*

She swallows, throat working as her eyes go wide with a mixture of anxiety and temptation. It's the look of a woman who went fishing for a minnow and hauled in a twenty-pound trout. I get it—I certainly didn't accept an invite from Saunders to hit 80s night at a cheesy dance club thinking I was going to meet someone like her.

But I did. *We* did.

And the fact that we're both here, thrown together by the surprise wedding of friends so close they're practically family, means something. If there's one thing my grandmother instilled in me aside from a hearty respect for the destructive power of love, it's that a man can't outrun destiny.

Fate brought Amanda and I here, and fate won't be satisfied until we live out whatever story it has planned.

After the ceremony, I give Mandy space, retreating to the bar to grab a beer while she's congratulating the happy couple, but I intend to corner her at the earliest opportunity. At least for the moment, my need to get her back in my bed is stronger than my respect for the dangers of the love box.

But when I turn back to the room, beer in hand, there's no sign of the woman in the black dress. She's vanished, the way she did the last time she danced into my life and my bed, only to turn to smoke by morning.

"Have you seen the maid of honor?" I ask Saunders, who is busy ordering a double shot of scotch to drown his recent breakup blues.

"Which one?" He jabs a thumb toward Brendan, our team captain and big brother of the bride. "The guy in the tiara is right there." He shakes his head with a disgusted sound. "I can't believe he wore that. The pictures are going to be all over social media before he gets to the parking lot."

"I meant the brunette," I say, old enough to know there are worse things than wearing a tiara for your sister's wedding. Like saying no to something that makes someone you love as happy as that tiara made Diana. "The one in the black dress."

Saunders growls low in his throat. "Don't, dude. Just don't. Trust me, it's the girl-next-door types who break your heart the hardest. They have no fucking mercy. None. At all."

"I hear you." I clap him on the shoulder, encouraging him to hang in there as I move away from the bar.

I prowl the party, search the empty hallway outside the skybox, and duck my head into the employee-only area, scaring the girls there sneaking a cigarette before they bring out more sandwiches, but there's no sign of Amanda. I return to the gathering, intending to ask Diana for more information on her friend, but abort the mission at the last minute.

If fate truly intended this chance meeting to lead to something more, it would have. If not, then tonight must be destiny's way of assuring me that I'm better off without passion in my life. It's a sign that I should look for a good friend I'd enjoy fucking to ease the loneliness that's made me a cranky bastard the past few months, instead of waiting around, secretly hoping lightning will strike a second time.

I don't need lightning. Lightning leads to the kind of heartbreak Saunders, with his sad, puppy dog eyes and tumbler of scotch, can't begin to fathom.

In the early days after Renee left, I couldn't even drag my body out of bed to fetch the vodka from the freezer. I was so fucking low I didn't even want to get drunk. Alcohol would have done nothing to numb my pain. The little girl we were going to name Sofia, after Baba, was gone. My fiancée had made it clear I was shit she couldn't wait to scrape from her shoe. And the happy future I'd been so sure of had crumbled in my hands, leaving only ash, bitter and sad, streaming through my fingers to blow away in the wind.

Thinking of those days, and how close grief came to wrecking everything I'd fought for since my mother sent me to boarding school in Minnesota so she could follow Mr. Bad Idea Number Two to a sheep farm in New Zealand, is enough to cool the heat seeing Mandy set loose in my bloodstream. I'm four, maybe six years away from retirement—if I'm lucky and one of the increasingly creaky parts of my body doesn't give out sooner—and I want to go out with a bang, not a whimper.

Besides, commitment to my team and my career has been proven to bear fruit. I've been a finalist for the Norris trophy the past five years—even won it once—and am on track to setting unbeatable defensemen records for the Badgers. All the relationship game ever got me was a battered heart and a bucketful of wasted time.

My head back in the game where it belongs, I say goodbye to my teammates, congratulate Nowicki and Diana on their marriage, and head for my car. I'm halfway across the staff lot, pulling my keys from my bag, when I spot a figure sitting on the ground beneath one of the lights in the adjacent parking lot. Even with the harsh light from above casting her face in blackness, I recognize Mandy immediately.

I'm already over the barrier between the lots, on my way to ask if she's okay, when she tips over, slumping onto her side. By the time I reach her still form, I've got 911 on the line.

"She's breathing, but she's out cold," I relay in a tense voice after I've given the dispatcher our location, my heart hammering as I check Amanda's pulse and find it swift, but strong. "I don't see any obvious sign of injury, but I didn't see her until she was already on the ground."

"An ambulance is on the way, sir," the operator replies. "Just stay where you are, don't move the patient, and keep her still and calm if she regains consciousness before help arrives."

"Got it." I brush Mandy's bangs from her pale forehead and gently probe the back of her skull, but there's no lump. Not a head injury, then—thank God. I'm debating whether to call Diana and tell her what's happened when sirens pulse through the still night. A moment later, spinning red lights are visible at the edge of the lot.

I wave my arm in a wide arc to make sure the driver sees us. A few heartbeats later, the ambulance skids to a stop beside us, and two paramedics leap out with a stretcher.

"Are you a friend?" A young woman with a long brown braid motions me out of the way as the other medics lift Mandy into the back of the ambulance.

"Yes," I lie. "I want to come with her to the hospital."

The woman nods. "All right, but you ride in the bucket seat by the doors. Buckle up and stay seated. We need you out of the way in case we need to treat her during transport."

I agree and hurry into the ambulance behind the brunette, buckling in as the doors slam closed and Mandy moans so softly I can barely hear her over the siren. But I catch the sound, and my gaze is fixed on her face as her lashes begin to flutter.

"She's waking up," I say, but the brunette is already leaning closer to Mandy's prone form.

"Amanda?" She puts a gentle hand on Mandy's arm. "Amanda can you hear me? You were found unconscious outside the arena and are on your way to the hospital. Can you tell me what happened, honey?"

"Oh no, not again," Mandy mumbles, brow furrowing. "I'm so sorry."

"Don't be sorry, sweetie," Brunette says kindly. "We just want to take care of you. Do you have any health problems we should know about?"

"Low iron levels," Mandy says in a weak voice. "But I'm taking supplements. My doctor said the fainting spells should pass in a week or two, probably by the time I'm in my second trimester."

"So you're pregnant?" Brunette asks as my inner voice lets out a long, low *fuuuuck* me, and silently admits that Mandy was right.

This is complicated. Crazy complicated. Even assuming she and her baby-daddy aren't together, I'm definitely not up for dating a soon-to-be mom. Relationships are hard enough when there aren't any innocent lives on the line.

Mandy sucks in a breath, and her hand flies to her ever-so-slight baby bump. "Yes, I am. Is the baby okay? I remember I sat down when I started feeling dizzy so I shouldn't have fallen far. And nothing hurts. But I shouldn't have left the party alone." Her eyes squeeze shut as she adds in a thick voice, "If she's hurt I'm never going to forgive myself."

"We'll get you and baby checked out at the hospital." Brunette motions to the shorter male paramedic, who makes a note in the paperwork he's filling out. "But I'm sure you'll both be fine. Do you know how many weeks along you are?"

"Twelve," Mandy says, the word a swift and sudden shock to my system.

At my fancy boarding school, I excelled at hockey first, literature second—years of listening to my grandmother's tall tales from the old country had made me a lover of stories —and math fifth or sixth, somewhere behind music appreciation and study hall. But you don't have to be a math genius to take today's date, subtract twelve weeks, and come up with a hot night in mid-July, which Mandy and I passed in very close company.

I'm running up against the truth hard and fast when Mandy's gaze suddenly shifts my way, as if she can hear the wheels screaming in my head as the gears turn too fast.

Our eyes lock for the second time tonight, and her jaw drops. "You... Oh dear."

Those three words transform my suspicion into certainty.

The baby is mine.

The baby is mine and simple is no longer an option.

> Puck Me Baby
> is out Fall 2017!

Printed in Great Britain
by Amazon